THE AUBU. ...ERENCE

—— *THE* ——

AUBURN
CONFERENCE

A NOVEL

BY TOM PIAZZA

University of Iowa Press • Iowa City

University of Iowa Press, Iowa City 52242
Copyright © 2023 by Tom Piazza
uipress.uiowa.edu

Printed in the United States of America

Design and typesetting by April Leidig

Printed on acid-free paper

Library of Congress Cataloging–in–Publication Data
Names: Piazza, Tom, 1955– author.
Title: The Auburn Conference : A Novel / by Tom Piazza.
Description: Iowa City : University of Iowa Press, [2023]
Identifiers: LCCN 2022040052 (print) | LCCN 2022040053 (ebook) |
ISBN 9781609388812 (paperback) | ISBN 9781609388829 (ebook)
Subjects: LCGFT: Novels.
Classification: LCC PS3566.I23 A93 2023 (print) | LCC PS3566.I23 (ebook) |
DDC 813/.54—dc23/eng/20220831
LC record available at https://lccn.loc.gov/2022040052
LC ebook record available at https://lccn.loc.gov/2022040053

For Mary, always

— **I** —

—1—

I HAVE COME TO the conclusion that the entire nation is insane.

Still, it is with a mixture of satisfaction, frustration, and hope that I, Frederick Olmstead Matthews, assemble for posterity this record of the events of June 1883 at the First Annual Auburn Writers' Conference, known to all now simply as the Auburn Conference. Sadly, of course, it was also the Last Annual Auburn Writers' Conference, for reasons that will no doubt be evident by the conclusion of this account.

If I were to have the opportunity to organize another such gathering . . . But I will abort this thought, as there is no such likelihood, and I have become convinced through many a season that we never do truly learn from our mistakes.

What is an American? This is the question that drove me mad.

In the late summer of 1882 I liked to walk along Mechanic Street by the Owasco River to clear my mind of gloomy thoughts. The bridge at Genesee Street was but a few blocks from the Institute, and my own modest rooms only another two blocks away. Crossing the river and turning south, I walked along a railroad spur and past a machine shop and a foundry, warehouses and a small mill, before the river finally widened and I could walk as far as the ice house, where I would cross again and make my way back toward the Institute. Quitting the center of town, seeing people at useful work, the proximity of water on its way somewhere . . . All were as necessary to me that year as oxygen.

The Institute—Auburn Collegiate Institute—sat on a pleasant few acres, equidistant from the New York State Prison (with its adjacent insane asylum), and the Home for the Friendless, so-called, which housed widows and indigents—collateral casualties of the late War between the States. These two landmarks might have served as the emblems of my mood that summer. For two years, I had answered to the title of Junior Lecturer in Rhetoric and English Literature at the Institute, where I was responsible for acquainting my first-year students with the canons of composition, rhetorical form, and grammar. In addition, I was assigned to deliver an introduction to the primary, and a few of the secondary, peaks and plateaus of English literature. I assembled a receiving line of the grandees of British letters—Chaucer, Shakespeare, Milton, Pope, Swift, Goldsmith, Dryden, Spenser, and so on. Each was awarded a few words of introduction and a handshake before the students were ushered down the line. Upper-level classes read these authors at length, if not in depth, along with the classics of Greek and Roman antiquity, but I, being of junior status, was relegated to the survey.

On two separate occasions during the year preceding, I had made the mistake at faculty gatherings of suggesting that our American literary production might be worthy of academic attention. I could as well have suggested installing a porcupine as the Institute's president. On the first occasion my idea met only a brisk dismissal. On the second I received a copious baptism in mockery, derision, and outright hostility. ("Yes—Let us study fishing yarns!" "Perhaps our text should be a catalogue of farm implements!" "Replace the Department of Music with instructors of the banjar!" And so forth.)

So I dutifully taught my young charges grammar, and I directed their fickle attentions toward the work of the antique figures on my list. But by evening lamplight I pored over the writings of Ralph Waldo Emerson, Walt Whitman, Herman Melville, and Mark Twain. Such independence of thought, such vigor in language, such engagement with the possibilities and challenges of the still-new country! "America . . . new-born, free, healthful, strong," wrote Emerson, in 1844, "the land of the laborer, of the democrat, of the philanthropist, of the believer, of the saint, she should speak for the human race. It is the country of the Future . . . a country of beginnings, of projects, of designs, and expectations." What a siren song!

I was but six years of age when our Civil War ended, raised in the North, and I assumed that our national argument had been settled, our future a glorious book yet to be written. My father managed a dry-goods store in Buffalo. He and my mother had emigrated from a nameless European backwater, sometime in the 1850s. They never spoke about that place, and I was discouraged from further inquiry. I had the impression that something terrible had happened there, the result of which being that America was for them a fresh start—*the country of beginnings*. The surname Matthews was apparently a fiction, likely a distillate from some unpronounceable Balkan patronymic. The sum of my father's wisdom, as imparted to me, consisted of this, half shouted over his shoulder as he stacked boxes: "Stop with the questions! Don't bother history, and it won't bother you." I took the advice to heart.

"The United States themselves are essentially the greatest poem," wrote Whitman, and I dreamed of plunging into the life of that great poem. I discovered my landmarks and moorings in books. In my imagination, I was Melville at sea, or Mark Twain on the river, or Whitman himself, containing multitudes. The authors were on fire with their visions, shaping a conception of the nation from those multitudes among which, surely, some role awaited me. I even imagined that I might one day add my name to their list. Unfortunately for that ambition I lacked any originality. Had I been reading Hawthorne? My style grew heavy with dread and the unpropitiated ghosts of England, the guilt of the Puritans. Had I just set down a volume of Twain? My prose coarsened and I started to sound like the old river man himself, rough as a camp skillet. A few leaves of Whitman's grasses and I was strong, able, confident, capacious, rich in adjectives, rich as well in adverbs, sublime, the necessary man. And Melville? All it took was a few pages aboard the *Pequod* and I sailed the empyrean, beheld the glow of the Indies and the dark significance of Leviathan, the exclamations and oaths of the hardy men at the yardarm!

I owned no traceable genealogy, and I resolved to construct a self from found elements, a "new-born, free, healthful, strong" person of my own invention—just as, one might say, the nation had. Because, like the nation, I did not know who I was.

Although as I came of age I had entertained the hope of entering Harvard, where I would dwell in halls that had housed Emerson and Thoreau, I was given to understand that we were unequipped financially—or socially—for such an aspiration. My view forward was directed away from Cambridge, and I was enrolled, at the age of seventeen, in Buffalo Normal School, to be trained as a teacher. I was a restless student, unsuited to methodical study; I responded instinctively to books, liked what I liked, avoided what I did not like. This is not the attitude with which to conduct a successful career as a student, and I managed to limp toward the end of my final semester and graduate *sine laude*. Shortly thereafter, in urgent need of a paying position, I accepted a perch as Junior Lecturer in Rhetoric and English at Auburn Collegiate Institute.

If I had had any hopes of discovering there an arena of vigorous discussion, of fresh ideas hotly debated by full-blooded colleagues, such hopes evaporated almost immediately. The students were put through their grey paces by grey-haired professors who were more preoccupied with the logistics of office assignment than with literature. Such intrigue regarding who sat with whom during faculty luncheons! Such readiness to bristle at slights, such capacity for nursing grievances!

As my second year of teaching at the Institute drew to a close, a cloud overtook me. Where was the bold conversation that I had hoped to find upon my emergence into the world? What was I doing with my talents, such as they were? And underneath those questions lurked something else—a nagging feeling of dread, having to do with America itself.

One had read spiritual and moral purpose in the books written in the years leading up to the Civil War. Every chapter, every line, was charged with meaning. The fate of the nation, of democracy itself, seemed to hang in the balance. Yet now, with the war not twenty years in the past, that sense of spiritual and moral urgency had dissipated. The accumulation of wealth had become the sole apparent purpose of every citizen. Railroads crossed the land, bridges spanned the rivers, factories and mills proliferated and generated unimagined profits, even as financial panics, labor riots, governmental corruption, and profiteering ran rampant. The southern states, with the North conveniently distracted by other matters, had returned their colored population to a condition near slavery in all but name. What were we doing with the freedom that had been won at such a cost? Was it no more than a license to enrich ourselves at others' expense? *The nation did not know what to do with its freedom.*

My students were indifferent to all of it. Almost to a one they had set their sights upon a safe berth somewhere—anywhere— overseeing the distribution of *this* among the merchants of *that.* . . . In that summer after my second year I must have walked a distance along the Owasco River equal to that between the Earth and the moon, turning these questions over in my mind. As summer closed and the new term opened I felt like a prisoner obliged to return to his cell after a brief interlude outdoors.

One afternoon in that September of 1882, while lecturing upon *Julius Caesar,* I grew so frustrated at trying to kindle a spark behind at least a few of my students' eyes that I found myself shouting at them, "Do any of you have an idea of what this drama is about?"

Several looked around to see if one of their number might offer some sort of response. Finally, Lemuel Fowler, who was a few years older than the other students, piped up and timidly offered, "They are going to kill the king, sir?"

"Yes. Yes, of course. But what is Shakespeare really driving at, here? What is the question they face?"

"Which conspirator shall do it, sir?"

"These are surface matters!" I said. "Underneath are questions all citizens must face! At what point is it necessary to break a law in order to affirm a principle? When must friendship be sacrificed for a higher ideal? Will you risk everything in the name of what you believe?"

Then, borne aloft upon this rhetorical tide, wanting to stir some emotional response in them, I recited the glorious words of the Preacher, from *Moby-Dick*:

Woe to him who, in this world, courts not dishonor! Woe to him who would not be true, even though to be false were salvation! . . . Delight is to him, who gives no quarter in the truth, and kills, burns, and destroys all sin though he pluck it out from under the robes of Senators and Judges.

The words must have been delivered with an uncharacteristic intensity, for the students regarded me as if I had taken leave of my senses. After a few more remarks, I read the clear decision in their faces. The instructor was defeated, and the class dismissed.

The next morning, while eating breakfast in the faculty dining room, I received a summons to the chambers of Elbert Olander, the chairman of the English Department. We had had an uneasy relationship since the day of my arrival at the Institute; he smelled insurrection in my doomed attempts to introduce the work of American authors into the curriculum. As I entered his office in Holyfield Hall, he faced me across his desk with an angry expression, his pointed nose, squinting eyes, and sharp, narrow shoulders giving him the look of a bird of prey.

"Matthews, we are engaged in the enterprise of producing young men who will be productive, responsible citizens, not anarchists."

"Sir?" I said.

"I am informed that you recited an anarchist speech in your literature class yesterday. Is this so?"

"*What?*" I responded, intelligently. "I conducted a discussion of the issues raised by the conspirators' predicament in *Julius Caesar*, and—"

"Issues?" he said. He picked up a sheet of paper from his desk, on which I could make out some handwriting, and he read from it. "'Be dishonorable . . . Burn, destroy . . . Kill senators and judges. . . .' I believe these were your words?"

"I was reciting a passage from *Moby-Dick*!" I said. "I was trying to illuminate the moral and ethical questions in Shakespeare's play—"

He stopped me with a raised hand. "Matthews," he said, "you are an instructor in literature, not in morals or ethics. Nor in theology, philosophy, or metaphysics. Nor, for that matter, in botany, astronomy, or metallurgy. *Literature.*"

What in God's name was that supposed to mean? "Shakespeare concerns himself with philosophy and ethics, doesn't he?" I said. "And Milton with theology. They raise questions with which everyone must struggle. Literature isn't just the making of pretty sentences—"

Olander stopped me again, fixing me with a cold glare. "If each person followed the dictates of his own impulses, or endlessly debated the rightness and wrongness of the regulations imposed by society, there would be no society. And if each faculty member made his own decision as to which rules he chose to follow at Auburn Collegiate Institute, and which not, there would be no Institute. And needless to add, I trust, you would have no employment." He sharpened his gaze. "Have I made my meaning clear?"

He had. He had indeed.

"From now on leave politics alone and confine yourself to literature." And with that he turned his attention to some papers on his desk.

I left Holyfield Hall and walked, seething, down Genesee Street, crossed the river, and headed south away from the town center. Confine myself to literature? He might as well have told me to confine myself to the sky, or the open sea. And anarchy! One man's freedom another's anarchy! What freedom, and for whom? Did not literature *hinge* upon that very point? I was beside myself; I may even have been ranting aloud as I walked. What would Emerson have had to say on that question now? Or Melville? Or

Whitman? I had only their pages, most written several decades before, which I had read over so many times that I could recite them from memory. I wished I could summon them in person, make them speak their minds, argue, debate. . . .

And with that wish arrived my great idea.

No—I will leave it to posterity to decide whether it was a great idea or pure folly.

Three days later I entered Holyfield Hall and was ushered into the chambers of Provost Wickham Moreland.

Moreland was practically a sovereign in the administration, with control of the Institute's financial choices and direction greater even than that of President Withers and the trustees. The Institute had narrowly escaped bankruptcy six years before, during the Panic of 1877. It had been rescued by Moreland—at the time a new provost, a flamboyant figure noted for an utter lack of interest in the school's educational mission and a keen preoccupation with his own profile among the city's social elite. Not the person to support my idea, at least not on the face of things.

The idea, which had seized me with the force of a vision in the desert, was to gather a group of writers at the campus for a public conversation about the future of America. A modern *symposium*—no less!—to be called the Auburn Writers' Conference. The possibilities had nearly overwhelmed me—I saw Walt Whitman reciting from *Leaves of Grass* on the stage at Midlake Auditorium, or discussing *Moby-Dick* with Herman Melville; Frederick Douglass and Harriet Beecher Stowe expounding upon the plight of the Negro . . . Mark Twain telling of travels across the country. . . . The Institute had facilities to host such a gathering, books could be sold. . . .

Yet the obvious hurdle had presented itself immediately. The only writers allowed in our sacred grove were those already safely embalmed. Chairman Olander would never agree to support the idea. God only knew what havoc living writers might cause! And, too, such a gathering would entail considerable expense. But it occurred to me that if I could make the case to the provost directly, convince him that what I envisioned would lend prestige to the Institute, and thereby to his reputation, I might be able to bypass Olander and the rest of his mummies entirely.

Of course there was no way to know whether my chosen writers would be available, or amenable to the idea, but I secured an appointment, and so, three days after my vision, I found myself in the offices of Wickham Moreland. He was installed behind a huge, ornate desk at the far end of a grand Oriental carpet; he made no effort to rise when I entered, merely gestured to a chair across from him. He wore a bright red and silver cravat and a waistcoat with a subtle trim around the lapels; his hair was steely grey mixed with waves of black, and carefully coiffed. The room was richly appointed, and I noted a complete absence of books lining the walls, which were dedicated to paintings of sailing vessels and hunt scenes.

When I was seated, he nodded as if to say "Proceed." I first thanked him for taking time to entertain my proposal, then I outlined my idea. The Auburn Writers' Conference would be an unprecedented gathering, including the most prominent American writers. It would consist not of a procession of individual lectures but of a series of conversations before an audience; the originality of this would add great interest to the event. I listed my proposed invitees; his eyebrows rose slightly at the mention of Mark Twain, which was encouraging. The presentations could be held at Midlake Auditorium, participants would be quartered at Harmony

House, meals taken at Founders' Hall. Books could be offered for sale, and a percentage remitted to the Institute. . . .

"Thank you," he said, halting my torrent. "May I ask why you have not applied to your department with this idea?"

"Sir," I began, "I have the highest possible respect for Chairman Olander and the English Department. Yet their concerns are focused—quite rightly, of course—on the past. They might support a lecture on Chaucer, but I doubt that such a program would attract a paying audience." He chuckled at this—another good sign. "The prospect of seeing Mark Twain and Frederick Douglass together on one stage, along with the authors of *Leaves of Grass* and *Uncle Tom's Cabin*, however, would catch the imagination of the Auburn community and beyond. The conference might, to use the phrase, 'put the Institute on the map' and ensure greater interest and investment from businesses and individuals who would regard the Institute in a new and brighter light."

I worried that the last remark might have been a step too far, but he gave no sign that might be the case. He was regarding me as if I were a previously unknown specimen of talking dog.

"You say that such a conference has not been attempted before?"

"Not to my knowledge."

He nodded. "Do these writers appear individually before the public for lectures and such? Do you know what they might expect as an honorarium?"

I had made a few provisional and largely baseless calculations as to likely expenses and receipts, and I told Moreland that I believed twenty-five dollars to be a reasonable guess. I watched him jot something down on a piece of paper and look at it for a moment, thinking.

"And have you any thoughts about likely potential receipts?"

"If we were to pay the participants a total of two hundred

dollars," I said, improvising, "and charge three dollars per person for attendance, even if we were to fill only a third of the auditorium's four hundred seats we would see a significant surplus. I expect we can do quite a bit better. And beyond that, the benefits to the Institute's prestige will bring much more significant rewards afterward."

He finished whatever he was writing down, surveyed it, and nodded twice.

"Intriguing," he said. "I doubt this could be achieved during the academic session, however. Our facilities are committed to the purposes for which they were designed. And the costs of renting facilities in the town would likely exceed revenues. Have you considered this?"

"I have," I said. "And it seems to me that the time to hold the conference would be immediately following commencement, in June of next year, when it might be easiest for any Institute personnel to extend their residence for, say, a week—students as well"—if any students were interested in anything beyond business receipts—"and merely keep the Institute's facilities open continuously for that extra time."

He regarded me full on, then, as if from a height, his lips pursed and some calculation taking place. "You do understand," he said, "that while I enjoy wide discretion in the matter of funding, I must submit any proposal, certainly one of this scale, to President Withers and the relevant department personnel."

I told him that I understood.

"There will be some resistance, I expect," he said.

I told him that I understood.

"Read me your full list of proposed participants."

I went down the list, and he wrote as I spoke.

"What about the man who writes the Uncle Remus stories?" he said. "My children love them."

At that moment my stomach sank through a previously invisible hole in the floor. Children's stories! But if agreeing to this was the cost of gaining his endorsement, it was not a mortal cost.

"That is an excellent idea," I said. "I will look into it."

"And you are willing to entertain other suggestions, and accept any strong objection to one or another of your proposed participants?" He looked at me, noticed my hesitation, raised his eyebrows, and said, "Say 'yes.'"

"Yes."

"Well said." He scribbled a few more notes, set his pen down, and said, "I will notify you of the outcome." I must have seemed dazed; perhaps he took it as disappointment, and he issued a smile that I took to be complicitous. "You might use your evenings to compose your letters of invitation."

Two days later, to my astonishment, a note arrived from Provost Moreland indicating that the president had agreed to my idea, and that they would arrange matters with Professor Olander at the English Department. "Absent yourself from the English Department offices for a few days until we have had an opportunity to mollify your chair."

And so the Auburn Writers' Conference was born.

In the following weeks and months letters were sent, underwriters conscripted among the city's business leaders, logistical plans drawn up, then modified, then modified again. Winter came and went in a blizzard of activity. Notices were written, to be placed in newspapers in Buffalo, Syracuse, Albany, Rochester, and Ithaca, as well as the Auburn *Guardian*. As springtime bloomed I was thrilled to receive positive responses from Herman Melville, Walt Whitman, Mark Twain, Harriet Beecher Stowe, and Frederick Douglass, all of whom expressed enthusiasm for the idea of the conference. The sole declining invitee was the author of the Uncle Remus stories, Joel Chandler Harris. He conveyed his regrets at his inability to make the trip north from Georgia, but he had taken the liberty of mentioning the invitation to one Forrest Taylor, a former Confederate general living presently in Richmond, who had published a memoir of the late war, and who, he was certain, would be a fine addition to our program, especially as he was an eminent representative of the South and so on.

I found this response somewhat presumptuous, but three days after Harris's letter arrived, a letter came from General Forrest Taylor himself, wittily acknowledging the awkwardness of the position in which Harris had placed both of us, and assuring me that if there were no place for him in the program he would take no offense, as he well understood why Mr. Harris would have been such an attraction. The letter was so disarming that I thought, well, perhaps a representative of the Southern cause should indeed be present. If the nation were to fulfill its destiny as a true Union, should not all points of view be taken into account? I wrote back that he would be welcome, and outlining the terms.

I was able to assemble a small army of assistants who could help in welcoming guests, checking off registrants, and escorting participants to their quarters and to events. In this, the departmental secretary, Miss Pound, was most helpful; one of her sisters, Lucretia, who was proficient in the Pitman method, volunteered to make a short-hand transcription of as many of the events as possible, which I thought would be an invaluable record. Another of her sisters was enlisted to stand at the doorway of the gala welcoming party we had planned for the participants and the town's elite, in order to keep away gate-crashers. And a friend of hers agreed to sell admission tickets to arrivals who had not purchased them in advance.

One morning, not a week after the exchange of letters with General Taylor, a note arrived in my box from Chairman Olander himself, asking if I might stop into his office as he had a request to make. That same afternoon I did so and encountered a completely different man than I had known, as if he had been replaced by a twin with an entirely opposite personality, an oddly equivocal aspect—almost deferential. He invited me to sit down.

"Well," he said, "Mr. Matthews, this is a request I think . . . well . . . I am certain that you would not imagine. . . . But here: My wife is a great reader, although our tastes do not always align, as one might say . . . and . . . well, I will put it this way: She is a great devotee of the novels of Lucy Comstock, and she has asked why her favorite author has not been included in the plans for the Writers' Conference. I am afraid that I made certain derogatory remarks about these books, of which as I say she is a great admirer, and we have not spoken for several days. . . . You see what I am saying, I hope. . . . If it were possible. . . ."

He was looking at me imploringly, with a pathetic aspect I had never seen in him. Lucy Comstock was a writer of popular romances, pure entertainment aimed at the simplest appetites of a wholly uncritical readership. She was a celebrity nearly on the order of Mark Twain, but her books had nothing to do with the questions to be considered at the conference. But as Olander spoke, two things did occur to me. Comstock would certainly attract paying attendees, which were necessary, and having Olander in my debt for such a favor was a cheque I might be able to cash on some future occasion. I told him I understood, and that I would do what I could.

"Thank you!" he said, with such emotion that I thought he might kiss my hand. "Thank you so much. Please let me know if there is anything I might do to help smooth your path."

I composed the desired invitation to Lucy Comstock. I was, admittedly, uneasy about the request. Now, if she accepted the invitation, there would be two participants out of tune with my initial conception. But if they helped make the conference a reality they would be welcomed.

And in any case, I told myself, look who would be participating: the authors of *Moby-Dick* and *Uncle Tom's Cabin*, of *The Adventures of Tom Sawyer*, of *Leaves of Grass*, and of the great *Narrative* written by the very oracle of the Negro aspiration toward freedom, Frederick Douglass. Who, if not they, could envision a more perfect Union?

—2—

"WHAT, PRAY TELL, is a 'writers' conference'?"

"You're a reporter," Hawley said. "Do your job and find out. Enlighten the populace."

Enlighten them, I thought, or put them into a narcoleptic trance. I picked up the sheet of paper from Hawley's desk, whence he had slid it across to me. The "news release" from the Auburn Collegiate Institute promised a "conversation about America," to be presented in two weeks' time. There followed a somber procession of mossy names—Herman Melville, Walt Whitman, Harriet Beecher Stowe. . . . Here was Frederick Douglass, who had been delivering the identical speech for forty years. Ah!—Mark Twain, a former newspaperman himself; at least he might say something worth excerpting for a quote. And this sentence: "Other participants include General Forrest Taylor and Miss Lucy Comstock." The lead, adroitly buried. The worthies of the ink-stained tribe were invited to contact Frederick Matthews, junior lecturer, et c, for details.

"Are you sure there isn't something a bit more lively that I might cover?" I asked Hawley. "Another drainage bill before the city council that I might review? Perhaps a new case of embalming fluid has been delivered to one of the funeral parlors?"

"We are the vision without which the people perish," he said, and spit an orange seed into a waste-basket several paces away. "Don't be a cynic."

"I am a reporter," I said. "They are synonyms. God help us on the day when reporters become anything but cynics."

Tardius sapientia est. . . . I could never remember the rest of it. The gist being "Wisdom is slow, but truth is fast." I had, so far, served a year and a half at the Auburn *Guardian*, and if truth were on its way it would doubtless have arrived already.

Nothing happens in Paradise—nor, be it said, in Auburn—not, at least, since the noble Brutus plunged the dagger into William Seward's breast—*thusly!* Even this had happened offstage, in Washington. It was as if the very trees and bricks had declared they'd had enough of drama. I arrived subsequent to the final curtain, having been passed over in my application for a position at the somewhat more dramatic Rochester *Tribune*. I was destined for larger things.

I thought I might at least spice up my item in regard to this "Writers' Conference" with a pithy quote or two from the honorable Lecturer Matthews. So on a lovely late morning in May I walked up Genesee Street, entered the grounds of the Auburn Collegiate Institute, followed my nose to one Holyfield Hall, and entered, accosting what looked to me to be a walking fossil, perhaps of the Silurian period, to ask where I might find Professor Frederick Matthews.

"Oh!" this skeleton exclaimed, taking a step backward. "He is, I believe, in the Department of English." He looked me up and down, perhaps puzzled that my head wasn't leaking sawdust.

"And, kind sir, the Department of English might be found . . . where?"

He pointed a finger attached to a palsied hand and intoned, "Th-there."

I thanked him and proceeded th-thereward. Lecturer Matthews,

I was relieved to find, was much younger than the Silurian I had just encountered; he looked positively youthful—beardless, and with a stubborn lock of hair that fell insistently over his brow, and which he forced back periodically with an impatient flourish of his hand. Very intense fellow, too, about the same age as myself. He sat at a small desk piled with paper, books, various writing implements, and other effects.

After a few words of introduction, I opened my notebook and said, "So, I have been enjoined to write a brief notice about your upcoming writers' festival, and I thought I might ask you to say one or two things that I could use in the notice to stimulate interest in attendance."

"Writers' *conference*," he said, then launched upon a lengthy diatribe, from which I managed to capture notes here and there on the wing, while most of the covey made its escape unmolested. It was all about America, and the War between the States, and the economy, and the writings of Emerson and Homer, and the Negro problem, and freedom and what freedom is and what freedom isn't. I had the distinct impression that I might have stood up and exited without his noticing. When he had finished I looked at my notebook page, where I had written *Books, Freedom, Negroes, America, War.* That ought to do it, I thought.

"Well," I said, shaking off sleep, "thank you very much. I am sure this will help attract a robust attendance. May I ask what you wish to accomplish with this gathering?"

He frowned, then looked down at his desk and tapped the end of a pencil against the wood rhythmically, five times, deep in thought.

"I would like to stimulate a conversation about serious questions," he said, "concerning the future of literature, and the future of the nation."

I finished my note, closed my notebook, and replaced my pencil in my jacket pocket. "Thank you very much," I said. "This will, I am sure, fill out my notice quite nicely."

I wrote the little news item for the *Guardian*, adding a few condiments to the recipe, and handed it to Hawley, who read it aloud as I stood at attention in front of his desk.

"'Partisans of Negro rights and Southern grievance are planning to square off, along with distaff proponents of women's suffrage, homosexual libertinism, free love, and literature, in a Battle Royale commencing on the fifteenth of June. . . .'"

He looked up at me from the page, and I could not tell if his expression expressed dismay or a wicked and complicit appreciation. He then continued to read the rest of it silently. Upon finishing, he asked, "Is this what the professor told you?"

"Lecturer, actually," I said.

"Is this in fact what he told you?"

"It is the essence of it," I replied, somewhat disingenuously.

"All right," he said. "Strike the part about the 'libertines' and bring this to Weems to set. Did you have something more in mind?"

"Well," I began, "I was thinking I might report on the conference itself. Write a feature article."

Hawley pursed his lips and peered at me. "You do realize," he said, dryly, "that we are in the business of reporting news, not manufacturing it."

"Yes, sir," I said, gravely. "Our readers depend upon it. And we, if I may say, depend upon them. To remain interested, I mean."

He emitted a sort of aborted laugh. "Oh, you are a card," he said. "I believe I was short-changing you by calling you a cynic." He began opening another of his oranges. "Goodbye. Stop at

Rebekah's desk on your way out and see if anything else of millennial import has come our way."

"Of course," I said. "And the feature? About the, uh . . ."

"Talk to me later in the week."

In order to report, you must have something to report upon. This tautology is inscribed upon the black heart of every newsman. I supposed there was something in the mere presence of these scribblers together in one room out of which one might have cooked up a more or less vegetarian side dish for the paper. Yet I was certain that ingredients might be added to attract the carnivores among the readership.

Did I have some ulterior motive in this thought? Yes, of course I did. Pulitzer's refreshed New York *World*, out of Manhattan, was a peppery alternative to the starchy maunderings found in the New York *Times* and its grey brethren. Its reporting was lively, focused on personalities and intrigues, rather than the tedious march of the quotidian. If excitement were in short supply, the editorship was clearly ready to do its part to help things along. I viewed the *World* longingly from my tidy dungeon in Auburn. I thought that if this "conference" could be painted in sufficiently bright primary hues, I might be able to place a notice in the *World*, and thereby secure a foothold by which I might lift myself up and out of Auburn.

So it was that two days later I rode west to the hamlet of Town Line, remarkable for being the only municipality in the Northeast to have seceded from the Union during the late hostilities. The population had held a referendum, in which the Unionists were defeated by a vote of approximately two to one. Street fights ensued. I imagined that all surviving parties to the dispute might be interested to know that a general of the Confederacy would be appearing on a stage alongside Frederick Douglass.

I made my way first to the Merchants' Bank, where I had learned that the former leader of the erstwhile secessionists was an officer. He greeted me suspiciously but warmed when I told him the purpose of my visit. "I do think," I said, "that perhaps General Taylor would benefit from the presence of as many adherents of the Lost Cause as might be able to make the trip to Auburn. No doubt Frederick Douglass intends to humiliate him publicly."

"Douglass!" he fairly growled. "Black devil. Write down for me the time and place. Here. . . ." He pushed a pen and a piece of bank stationery toward me, with his hand shaking, and I wrote down the specifics for him. "We will have a delegation to greet him!"

I stopped into several other establishments where I thought interest might be kindled, in each case presenting the notice in as neutral a fashion as possible until I could spy out the listener's sympathies. There were more than a few opponents of the town's secession still bitter about the twenty-year-old schism, including the proprietor of Bruder's Bakery, where a flour-covered apparition in a white apron confronted me with a raised spoon, promising to give that Confederate scofflaw a personal beating. I tried to soothe him, but I did not try very hard. I had to repeat the exact hour and location for him three times.

On my way back to Auburn I visited Seneca Falls, where was held the women's rights convention of 1848, wondering if I might find some pot worth stirring—perhaps a temperance militia at drill practice, or a Suffragist bake sale. Only ghosts populated the Wesleyan Chapel, where the meeting had been convened those thirty-five years past, and visits to various churches, banks, saloons, and dry-goods shops yielded nothing. But at last by pure luck I found at the Universalist Church an afternoon social gathering of rather formidable women, under the rubric of the Seneca Women's Committee. Two of them were, in fact, from Auburn. I told them of the upcoming debate in Auburn. One woman, the apparent leader of the group, asked me why there had been included no advocates of women's suffrage.

"I should think that would be an excellent question to pose at the conference itself," I replied. I informed them as well of the promised appearance of Mrs. Stowe and Miss Comstock at the conference. The latter name provoked the most astonishing variety of responses. "Trivial stories full of docile females, dependent upon men for their lives!" one exclaimed, to loud assent from most of the others. Yet several in the group betrayed an initial excitement, which they made haste to conceal. As a group they vowed to attend and ensure that the flag of women's rights would fly high during the conference.

Back in Auburn, I composed and dispatched a letter to the New York *World*, apprising them of the impending cataclysm and suggesting that I might be uniquely situated to report upon it. This done, I strolled around town and took note of the public notices posted for the event, all modest and straightforward, printed in neat and orderly letters, tacked up at the Presbyterian church on Franklin Street and in a few other places. They seemed rather anemic, so I took the liberty of designing a large poster of my own; I had Weems's boys in the printing area set and print twenty of them, and I placed them myself in spots where I judged they might have the most effect. I oversaw the typography, and was rather proud of the result.

COMING!

I affixed these masterpieces to every prominent and sensible surface I could find—taverns, City Hall, outside churches and schools, the police and fire stations—and afterward I returned to my daily round of police blotters and street repair notices to await the coming of the Apocalypse.

—3—

AT TWELVE MINUTES past four on the afternoon of Thursday, June 14, 1883, a man in late middle age, with a full, well-trimmed beard and intelligent eyes that seemed to regard everything across a great distance, stepped down from the train at Auburn, foregoing the conductor's proffered assistance. One small valise followed him, carried by a porter, whom he tipped generously. Once clear of other descending passengers, he stood looking up at the cloudless late-spring skies and the trees, absent-mindedly fingering the large copper one-cent piece given him by his grandfather, which he carried in his left trouser pocket along with a small and well-worn length of whalebone. It had been a while since Herman Melville had made a landing, alone, in an unfamiliar city.

He had not yet firmly decided to attend that evening's gathering, an embarkation party for the week-end's event. Such gatherings had become uncomfortable for him; in recent years he had tentatively accepted, then withdrawn from, more than one such invitation. His early successes, nearly forty years in the past and based on his first-person accounts of travels in the South Seas, he thought of now with ambivalence. He considered them minor works and chafed under the lingering general view that he was no more than a weaver of such romances. The public remembered him, if they remembered him at all, as the barefoot narrator of *Typee*, likely lost, by now, to the cannibals. Since the indifferent reception afforded *Moby-Dick*, the book he considered his finest achievement, and the scorn heaped upon two subsequent novels, he had withdrawn from a literary world that seemed to lack any further use for his talents.

A deepening pessimism about human possibility had rested heavily upon his spirits in these later years, and at intervals his family and closest friends had even feared for his sanity. He worked long, tedious days at the Custom House in New York City, conducting dreary rounds and compiling lists. When a letter arrived inviting him to participate in a symposium of writers, he was deeply unsettled and had initially rejected the idea. But the prospect of such a gathering, after so long a period of isolation, stimulated anticipation along with the reflexive anxiety. He had decided, finally, with lingering misgivings, to accept the invitation.

Five minutes after quitting the train, he found himself seated in a carriage across from a man perhaps ten years his junior, quite handsome and dressed in an elegant jacket and shined boots. Melville asked the man if he were participating in the conference.

"I am," the man replied. "I imagine you are as well?" Melville noticed a three-inch scar below and to the rear of his left ear.

Melville replied in the affirmative and they introduced themselves; the man's name was Forrest Taylor.

"Melville the author of *Typee*?" Forrest Taylor asked. Melville noted the appraising aspect of the man's expression, the eyes a mixture of irony and arrogance above a thin, unkind smile.

"Yes," Melville said. He apologized to Taylor for being unfamiliar with his work, and asked what he had written.

"A personal memoir of the War of the Secession," Taylor replied. "I was a general of the Confederacy." After a pause apparently designed to measure the effect of this information on Melville, he added, "I was rather surprised the invitation was extended."

"I was surprised as well," Melville said. "About my own invitation, I mean."

"How so?" Taylor said.

"I doubted that anyone remembered my books," Melville said. "Most have been out of print for years."

"Then we are lodge brothers," Taylor said, evidently pleased. "Relics of past glories."

The remark, and the satisfied smile that accompanied it, contained a quality of implied complicity that made Melville uneasy, and he was relieved when the carriage entered the gates of the Auburn Collegiate Institute.

Having been aided up the stairs at Harmony House by one of the students, a boy named Lemuel, to whom he gave a half dollar in gratitude, Walt Whitman lay back on the bed pillows and closed his eyes. The windows were open, and a slight breeze carried the scent of mown grass in to him. June was an empire of fair promise.

Old age is the time of ebbing—memories, powers of reason, fluids, ambitions. He had wished to contain all. But soon, he knew, all would contain him. Reaching for his jacket, which he had thrown on top of his bag on the floor near the bed, he retrieved a small notebook from the inside pocket and wrote down this thought, then set the notebook and pencil on the nightstand.

His doctor had advised against any lengthy excursion, yet the prospect of speaking at a college was enticing, as if he had been offered a temporary visa back to the land of youth, and he had come, a long and unpleasant trip from Camden. The college, he had been told, was out of session now. He wished he could have heard the shouts of the boys at play, seen them hurrying with their books to class, golden-haired or brown-haired or black-haired, tanned by the sun and strong in their youth, happy on the playing field and happy also in the dining hall, calling out in names of friendship, jesting, contending in games of skill. . . .

He was hungry. Was it ever enough? No, and may it never be

enough. How much beauty there was, and so fleeting. The word "freedom" had caught him in the invitation letter. Its meaning had begun to turn in the preceding few years, taken on a sinister drift—"sinister" meaning left-handed, of course. Just as "influence" was the pouring-into, and "prophecy" the bubbling forth . . . Words were wings; they lifted you. At the same time, they sent their roots deep into the loam of the human mind and tethered you. . . . He was growing agitated. . . . "Supercilious" was a raised eyebrow, "prurience" an intolerable itch.

He closed his eyes again and resolved to quiet himself and rest in advance of that evening's gathering.

Mark Twain fished a cigar out of his inside left breast pocket as the countryside west of Hartford opened out and the river flickered behind the fine elm trees. He found the trimmer in his other pocket. His presence had caused a fuss at the station; small crowds, turning toward him like schools of fish. He dispensed a few words, which he forgot immediately. Mrs. Stowe, his traveling companion, stood to one side, annoyed and somewhat envious. He joked her out of it as they boarded. He had given an autograph to the conductor.

They look at you and you look at them. The you who looks at them is not the you they see when they look at you. Iron law of life right there. Mr. Clemens behind the window in the back office, keeping the accounts for his front man. He was used to being the most famous person in the room. Was this why he struck the nostalgic note so often? Back when the exchange was straightforward and they liked you or didn't like you because they liked you or didn't like you. Much more like regular billiards—three balls on the table, the pure geometry. Flawed comparison; you can't blame the other balls for getting in the way. . . .

Dozing, and rocking. Sunlight stuttering in the window from between the majestic elms. That river that pressed on him from inside. What had been freedom at a certain age became necessity later on. Another iron law, rusting with the years . . . The porter had stashed the boxes of books; this question woke him, briefly, and he remembered. Stuttering, like a drum tattoo. Stowe across the aisle. Remembered the little Negro girls in San Francisco, skipping rope, laughing and chanting,

> Chinky Chinky Chinaman, sitting on a fence;
> Trying to make a quarter out of fifteen cents . . .

He used to keep a notebook with that stuff, a harlequinade of social types; now he could summon it at will, from memory . . . did it in the river book and now the raft . . . tragedians, card sharps . . . Natchez under the hill . . .

When he awoke they were near Watertown; his watch said 5:37. Sky still light, nearing the apogee of spring's upswing. They had dinner brought to their car while the train took on water and the other necessities. How was it possible that for every dollar he made he got five dollars further into debt? A medicine show barker, selling his own daydreams. Any fort became a jail eventually, even your own face.

How hard could it be to cook a bird on a train? Her capon was underdone, bloody at the bone. Across the aisle, Twain had fallen asleep, and she eyed the remains of his beefsteak, debating whether to annex it. He had talked her into coming despite her misgivings, despite the fact that she could no longer bear to hear anyone's opinion about anything. Twain jollied her up, told her jokes; she could stand to be around him, at least.

She managed all her household affairs, supervised the staff, wrote the books, settled the accounts, accepted speaking engagements, and could still cook any bird with her eyes closed without dripping blood all over the floor. *Uncle Tom's Cabin* had made her family wealthy, for a while. It still pulled the cart, despite the stupidities that had been stitched together by countless minstrel troupes and theatricals from the fabric she'd woven, and from which stupidities she realized not a copper penny. She herself was the last person left with whom she took pleasure in conversation. Wasn't that right, Mrs. Stowe? Absolutely, Mrs. Stowe. She had no idea why she had been invited to this gathering or what she was supposed to say. Twain told her that Frederick Douglass was coming; that was a reason to show up, despite the advertised presence of the twittering Comstock. The entire gathering seemed not just improbable but unreal, and she was preoccupied with many things, but she had agreed, and it did not seem as if it would be too great a transgression if she were to free that small portion of steak from its unresolved destiny amid Twain's snores, before it got cold altogether, and, keeping one eye on his face and another on his plate, she extended her arm, fork poised for the deed.

The westering sun glared through another train window, disappeared, reappeared. Orchard-heavy June; leaves backlit in the cloudless afternoon, rivers and fields, past Utica toward Syracuse and beyond. Frederick Douglass stared out at the countryside. Through his mind ran the little song he had written, and which no one had ever heard. It was not so much a song as a rhyme, with a little tune he had conceived, and which he hummed quietly. . . .

> Frederick Bailey's here and gone;
> Frederick Douglass wrote this song.

Sings it fast, sings it slow,
But where did Frederick Bailey go?

Douglass pulled his watch from his vest pocket, checked it, replaced it. In his jacket, near his heart, he carried a miniature book of Robert Burns's poems, which he had purchased in Scotland and kept with him because it reminded him of happier times. He had agreed to this week-end's invitation hoping, perhaps, to capture a chimera, a most elusive fellowship, the proximity of writers with whom he might even for a few hours be a Writer, and not a Representative.

He was born to the Peculiar Responsibility—accepted it, dedicated his life to it, and it bore down upon him incessantly. If he could have shed it, like a snake's skin, would he have done so? What, if anything, would be left inside the skin? He had transformed himself into a Protagonist—*the* Protagonist—who would stand for an entire people, shaped and cured in the light of repeated tellings. Yet the boy he had been—the boy he had never had a chance to be—had slipped away, escaped under cover of narrative.

He traveled constantly, preaching the gospel of freedom, as if freedom were the end in itself. It had to be *made* an end in itself—one needed to sharpen the point, temper the blade, in order to penetrate the hearts of listeners. Yet in private hours he wrestled with the angel, demanding an answer to the question of what to do with freedom once it arrived. And the angel, wrestled to a standstill and faced with the question, would disappear, leaving only a disembodied laugh hanging in the air. . . .

The hotel soaps always smelled of lye. Cora was to make sure that her personal lavender soaps (French-milled) were lined up a certain way, and her wardrobe arranged so that choices could be made at a glance. The windows of Lucy Comstock's room afforded a view from the third floor across Genesee Street and into a little park. She was annoyed to find no hotel stationery in the tiny escritoire, and she had Cora call down to the front desk for some so that she could attend to correspondence before getting ready for the evening's gathering.

The conference organizer had offered her a room at something called Harmony House, which she had declined with a request to secure a suite in the town's best hotel, the Owasco, a very ugly name. Early in her career of producing immensely popular, and profitable, novels, Lucy Comstock had determined that she would accept only first-class accommodations; it did no good to her reputation to play the modest, humble female in need of help and charity. It was a lie, in any case. The only help she needed she received from Cora, and when that had been provided she needed . . . nothing.

There were more than a few who thought her a scarlet figure, as she made no pretense of either chastity or domestic submissiveness. The irony was that the women in her novels were all in search of a strong man to whom they might submit in matrimony, a character type utterly opposite to her own. They had graciously made her fortune. She was well versed in the heady, sensuous details that could transmit a thrill; she had a shrewd, definitive, unsentimental grasp of her readers' underlying fears and hopes, and she provided the narratives that piqued their appetites and soothed their misgivings and, finally, assured them that all would be well in the end.

Her publisher had sent the boxes of her books, which were to be on display and for sale at the location of the "conference." Why she had been invited to this gathering was a mystery to her. She had tried to tease out some hidden motive, to see if she were being somehow set up for ridicule, yet the response from the organizer,

Matthews, had been so direct and ingenuous—he knew that her presence "would attract enthusiastic attendees"—that she had agreed. But she would impose her own story of who she was in contrast with all these weighty male names, these Titans who dealt with "large," ponderous themes. She imagined them as an array of wax figures in a museum. She would melt them.

—4—

My Dear Duyckinck—

How I wish you could have been alive to attend this evening's event. I am writing by a wavering candle in my room at "Harmony House," guest quarters on the campus. The "welcome party" earlier tonight was stimulating for ten minutes, then a burden under which I slowly sagged for another half-hour before I slunk off to my chamber.

On this afternoon's ride from the depot to the Auburn Collegiate Institute I was welcomed into the fraternal order of has-beens by a Confederate general who seemed pleased to meet the barefoot author of *Typee*. He has apparently published a long narrative complaint and opined that we are both of us relics of a glorious and vanished past! The Whale has sounded in earnest, apparently, and shows no sign of resurfacing.

I had not met Whitman until tonight. We are to be the opening speakers at the presentation tomorrow morning. He manifests the strangest mixture of abundant self-regard and near complete lack of affectation. The history of his visits to the food table could be charted by the crumbs in his beard, and his dress was loose and quite careless. Yet even this evident disregard for outward appearance seemed somehow calculated to produce an effect. One cannot help but be charmed, up to a point. He was the spirit of garrulous bonhomie among the town's civic eminences, yet he displayed a degree of discomfort or wariness in our own exchanges, as if we were generals on opposing sides who were to meet in battle the next morning.

Possibly I am overstating the awkwardness. Mark Twain is here, surrounded by a coterie of petitioners for his attentions, and we had time for a cordial handshake and not much more. It was, I will admit, gratifying beyond my expectations to be recognized by other writers, after assuming that I had been well forgotten. The organizer of the affair, Matthews, was embarrassingly effusive in his greeting. He seems awfully young to me, but then nearly everyone here seems awfully young to me.

I should have mentioned Frederick Douglass. We had not previously met, although we had been around New Bedford in the same years. He greeted me with exceptional warmth, and we conversed for some minutes—he, like Twain, had a line of petitioners, but unlike Twain he did not appear to regard them as the evening's main attraction. At any rate—what a rare being he is. A mixture of extraordinary warmth and intelligence with something steely inside—or perhaps it was the other way around. His aspect shifted as one talked with him, like a moon going through its phases. I was truly moved by his words about my books, especially *Benito C*, which modesty forbids me to enshrine in this epistle. . . .

I will close now, and perhaps I will find you in a dream.

Yrs,
HM

When Melville had finished writing the letter to his departed friend, a nightly ritual, he folded the paper and placed it in his travel bag. There was sufficient life remaining in the candle for him to be able to look over some notes he had been making toward a new novel. "Notes" was a somewhat misleading word; he had, unaccountably, found it impossible to proceed beyond the first line. Each day this line changed, often several times in a sitting, each instance a lunge at some elusive ghost of possibility. Three words could suffice, if they were the right words—this he had proved. He kept a notebook with these lines, to which he added almost every night, with instructions for his wife to burn it upon his death.

A slave named Orestes laid the cornerstone of the house;
    he was my grandfather.
There is a beetle out of whose crushed wings is made a beautiful
    dye.
When the snows fell that year the streets of Lakeland were
    buried in silence.
No one could have predicted the ascendancy of Horace Wacker.
"So!" Edwina said. "Two desserts were not enough for you!"
A decision was necessary, and a meeting was called.
How was it possible for two sisters to be so unalike?
Everyone knew there had been trouble at the blacksmith shop.
The choice had been narrowed to three, and there was no one
    left to deliberate.
The train was late arriving, so Ethan ordered a second whiskey.
In the city of Lakeland lives a man who changed history.
Force of habit, he thought—nothing more.
Jonathan Blight would always remember the expression on his
    aunt's face at the funeral.

It was a different book every day, and a different writer. Prose narrative was consuming itself. He had written poems, published at his own expense excepting one or two fugitives for which a tiny ransom had been paid, but otherwise he had driven straight into the densest thicket of contending visions, the colors which, when projected together, fused into a single bright, white light, the dissolution of finite consciousness, ambiguities which became microscopically granular. . . . There were days when he imagined himself the very embodiment of the madness of civilization itself. Was any coherence possible if one dwelt among impossible contradictions? He had come to the end of what he had to say. Was it then a heresy to continue to speak? He felt the slow undertow again, the slant of shadows outside Jerusalem, night coming on, spreading like blood from a wound, oil lamps and *houris*, red draperies, hideous doubt, the panic of Mar Saba, no border in any direction, futility of desert, open door, pyramid shadow, even without the casing, the labyrinth, evaporation or burial, unanswerable question . . . shaking with shame . . . He would leave the next morning; he would sit at the depot and wait for the next train to carry him home. This had been a mistake.

Ti gaziki la mama ba zameena; ma eh subiki caboomba bonzo gabballa . . .

Mark Twain poured himself two more fingers of Scotch as he read over the words he had written. At *"gabballa"* he began to laugh and fell into a coughing fit. He recovered himself, replaced the bottle on the tray in his room at Harmony House, and relit his cigar. If he could have done so, he would have authored and published an entire volume of pure gibberish, nonsense syllables, written in a nonexistent grammar from some sunken continent of his mind. Out of the question, obviously—anyone reading it would conclude that he had finally gone nuts.

The prize of the evening's gathering had been encountering Frederick Douglass for the first time, the one person in the room whose renown might have exceeded his own. A certain recognition of this fact seemed to pass, unspoken, between them and put them both at relative ease. Nobody who did not live behind the mask of fame could truly understand that recognition. Well, he thought, that was not entirely true; every Negro he had ever met lived with that double citizenship. Some had been more willing to lift the mask, briefly, than others, understandably. He had invited Douglass to share some brandy and cigars the next night. Douglass had seemed anxious to find someone with whom he could relax. Charm, and underneath it a tremendous tension.

Or, he thought, he could write a book composed only of sharply rendered, disconnected images, like the objects found by chance in the dirt when you were a boy. Focused on the world before you, in miniature, each encounter charged with mystery and wonder. Accompanying him on this trip, as on every other, was a hand-tooled leather valise he had acquired in San Francisco, full of such small talismans. A translucent blue glass bottle, the aquamarine color delicate as a veil, caked with mud. Or an arrowhead, an ancient coin, a marble, shards of crockery, clay pipes: each a fragment of some beautiful ruin. Instead of the façade, the errands, the correspondence, just an image—a pocket knife, a magic rock—the true, unwritten story of his life.

Late that same night, Frederick Douglass wrote in his diary:

This evening I met Herman Melville. Knowing I was to see him at this event, I had revisited *Benito Cereno*, his masterpiece, and marveled again at his insight into the mechanism of deception and treachery necessary to maintain control of a population of enslaved men, the barbarity that is made inevitable. . . . Not just the fact, but the grim irony attending it—the way in which the mechanism makes prisoners of all concerned. "You are saved," Captain Delano exclaims, and the question, "What has cast such a shadow upon you?" And Don Benito's simple and chilling response, "The negro."

It is an irony upon which to choke in perpetuity. The shadow falls upon the master, yet were I to be posed the same question, I should have to give the same answer, as would every Negro I know. To those who consider our titular freedom under law to be the settling of the case, and who suppose us to be now "saved" . . . what has cast such a shadow upon us?

Leaving aside the savage dismantling of the Negro's prospects in the South, the renewed impediments to education, economic advancement, and the franchise, whence the shadow? If I were to have the riches of all Byzantium, and the entirety of world literature committed to memory, and if I owned mansions in every capital of the world, were I to enter into conversation with a white man, even the most well-meaning white man—*especially* the most well-meaning white man—that conversation would turn, inevitably, to the question written on my face, of my color, and my thoughts about my color, and my feelings about my color, and the situation of others of my color, and how am I able to stand the injustices, and what are my thoughts on the Ku Klux, and what can they, as especially well-meaning white men, do. . . . All reasonable questions, inevitable questions, all concerning me *only as a representative of a group*, never an individual—all seeing only The Negro, and never the man. And in this I have been *complicit*, of necessity, for only in advancing the abiding dilemma of the Negro *qua* Negro can the necessary awareness be generated, and the necessary pressure brought to bear. The shadow, the dilemma itself, becomes the mechanism of survival and progress. It has been forced upon every man and woman of my race, like Dumas's iron mask.

Melville sees through the mask, yet I could not help but wonder what mask he himself wore, and for whom. He had the air of one who had suffered a wound that imposed a necessary barrier between himself and the world. At any rate, nothing I have ever read has shown such a grasp of the infernal trap in which the slave master places not only his slaves but himself, and the tragic distortion and perversion of self in which the slave must operate in order to survive.

Twain was of all the most agreeable in person. He wore his own renown as a sort of mask, but when meeting one-to-one regarded me as if we shared not a tragic secret but a joke. We passed an invigorating few minutes before others enforced our public roles upon us once again, and he suggested that we find time at some point during the week-end to share brandy and cigars away from the attendees.

The only unpleasant note was the presence of "General" Forrest Taylor, an invidious Confederate apologist, the apotheosis of the aggrieved Southern white man, who sees all the hypocrisies of the North yet claims never to have laid eyes upon a white-robed Klansman, the putative hallucination of the Northern abolitionist. I was not aware that he had been invited. Young Matthews, the organizer of the conference, pointed him out to me, and when I asked about the rationale for his presence, Matthews stammered out words to the effect that he hoped to present "all sides." I let this pass without response.

————

And at a modest rooming house a few blocks from the Institute, after letting down her dark red hair, a woman neither young nor old prepared for bed, flush with a previously unsuspected audacity. In her notebook she had written the words *HOME FOR THE FRIENDLESS*, which she had seen on the lintel above the doors to a large house she had passed while walking earlier that day. She could hardly contain the excitement, an amalgam of desperation and exaltation. Over the long years, she had become the private virtuoso of a species of control which had, finally, come to control her. This week-end was an experiment, a kind of raid, as she thought of it—unprecedented and never to be repeated—to regard directly the world and its obscure intentions.

She read over the letter she had written to her sister:

Dearest Vinnie—

You must not tell anyone this, but I have stolen away for two days in order to attend a "Writers' Conference" in Auburn, New York. It was an eight-hour journey by train and I am quite exhausted. I bribed Chips with the promise of a special cake which I will bake him upon my return. I thought that if I made no fuss I should be able to slip out and in with ease. O, I am excited! With all the dying around us I have resolved to let life approach close so that I may at least touch it—feel its pulse. Do not think harshly of me for placing the burden of this secret on you!

E

— **II** —

— 5 —

IN THE DEEP RECESSES of upstate New York the winters are empty and absolute as the desert; the wind, the cold, the buried earth, black branches and chimneys etched sharp against an endless bone white. When spring arrives, and then the summer, the richness of the orchards, the vineyards, the lakes and trees and fauna, the high spirits in paddle boats and carriages, can make you forget the winter and its desolation, and one can believe oneself in Paradise until autumn in its treacherous glory erodes that certainty and by November closes the lid on the world of appearances, driving one indoors, even underground, once again. It is a territory of extremes.

Auburn sits at the geographical center of a region referred to as the "Burned-over District," which runs roughly parallel to the route of the Erie Canal, grazing the upper tips of the Finger Lakes, between Albany and Buffalo. In the early decades of the nineteenth century, pioneers from New England made their way west through this territory, founding small farms and observing uneasy treaties with the native Iroquois and Mohawk. They brought their religion with them, along with its contentious denominations—Presbyterian, Methodist, Congregational, Baptist, Universalist—and missionaries followed them on horseback distributing pamphlets and Bibles. But, like the desert, the land engendered prophecy, and in the isolation of the scattered early settlements sects splintered and proliferated, animated by warring convictions regarding man's responsibilities on Earth, the prospect of endless punishment for sinners, and the possibility of salvation.

By mid-century the region was a spiritual *aurora borealis*, vibrating with theories, experiments, visions, and madness. Mormonism, Shakerism, Perfectionism, Adventism, strict sexual abstinence, epic polygamy, communal living experiments, and great social movements charged with the volatile energies of religious fervor—abolitionists, suffragists, fugitive slaves finding temporary refuge in cellars and barns on their way to Canada. Lone prophets on fire with idiosyncratic readings of Scripture roamed the streets and roads and fields, gathering adherents ready to follow anyone who delivered a bold certainty and a compelling narrative in stirring oratory. In communities and towns with names reaching back to antiquity—Ithaca, Homer, Seneca, Ovid, Virgil, Cato, Romulus, Hector, Brutus, Ulysses—an idealized, mythic past shared the imagination with a millennial future. It was the present that posed an insoluble riddle.

A discreet knock on the door awakened Herman Melville. After a moment he said "Thank you" and sat up in bed. Outside, honeyed sunlight filtered through the oak trees and across a patch of lawn at the Auburn Collegiate Institute, and although it was mid-June the air was cool and pleasant. He found himself at once in an altogether different mood than the one that had unnerved him the night before. The sky above Harmony House was as fickle as the sea, he thought, and his mind as fickle as either.

He prepared himself for the day, dressed, and thumbed through the copy of his book-length poem *Clarel*, which he had brought with him, searching for a passage to read at the morning's presentation. The seven years between the book's publication and this visit to Auburn had done nothing to quicken the public's interest in *Clarel*'s eighteen thousand lines of verse, an epic meditation on civilization in the form of a series of conversations among a group of travelers during a journey to the Holy Land. The book had met with a resounding silence worthy of the Dead Sea itself. Aware that the morning's event would pair him with Whitman and that poet's booming optimism, Melville gravitated to the sections spotlighting Ungar, the wounded former soldier who foresees nothing but doom for democracy and mankind.

Walt Whitman, awakened in his room at the opposite end of Harmony House by an identical knock, called out "I am." For some seconds he was unsure of where he was. Slowly he came to himself. He realized that he had issued an inappropriate response. The Latin *ego sum* . . . but appropriate enough, he thought. If all his work might be summed up in two words, surely those were the two. He added the words "Thank you," although the student who administered the knock had proceeded to his next assigned door. In no hurry to rise, Whitman lay under the sheet, gazing out the window at the rich morning light and the still-damp lawn. He had an erection. Lazily, happily, he attended to it.

Carriages began arriving at Midlake Hall that Friday morning well in advance of the ten a.m. start time. In the Midlake lobby a dozen or so browsers examined stacks of books that had been arranged on two long tables by a local bookseller, Mr. Widge, from Ganseltown. Inside the auditorium itself attendees made their way through the long rows of narrow, leather-upholstered wooden seats arrayed in shallow arcs radiating back and under a balcony supporting seven more rows, at the rear of which the morning sun spilled through a large, circular window.

On the stage at five minutes before the hour, behind a long table draped with an ochre-colored cloth, Walt Whitman, Herman Melville, and Frederick Matthews sat awaiting the beginning of the Auburn Writers' Conference. Whitman wore a huge, high-crowned felt hat, broad-brimmed, the size of a Mexican sombrero; he smiled through his flowing white beard and nodded at audience members as they filed in. Melville sat next to him at the far end, still paging through *Clarel*. In the seat nearest the lectern, Matthews read through the notes for his opening remarks, which he had been awake revising since before dawn.

A few minutes earlier, he had been detained by Lemuel Fowler just as he reached the steps to mount the stage.

"Sir," Fowler had said, nervously, "There's a man who says he must speak to you." With an inclination of his head Fowler indicated the individual, who was standing several feet away, and Matthews recognized, to his dismay, a local character who called himself, variously, King Prince Nommo and Rabbi Ben Ezra. On most days the man could be found on street corners haranguing the storefronts and handing out crudely printed tracts of impenetrable Jeremiac spleen. Matthews had tried to be polite in their odd encounters, but the man always wanted something. The hall was filling.

"I am about to begin the program," Matthews hissed at Fowler, but the man had already approached. He wore a turban with the image of an eye in the middle of the forehead.

"*Doctor*," the man said. This was his habitual greeting when they met, and Matthews had given up correcting him.

"Hello, Rabbi," Matthews said. "Can this wait until—"

"I am the Prophet Ben Hamouda," the man said.

"Yes, of course," Matthews said. Yet another incarnation. "I'm sorry. But I must begin the proceedings. Can this—"

"I wish to address the multitudes," the Prophet said, gesturing with one hand toward the audience.

"Look, Prophet, can you find me later and we can discuss your idea?"

"Now is the now of now," the Prophet replied.

"Unquestionably," Matthews replied. "But . . . please." And, not waiting for a reply, he turned and mounted the stage.

At the striking of the hour, with the hall two-thirds full, the signal was given, the doors to the lobby were shut, and, drawing a long, deep breath, Frederick Matthews rose and stepped to the lectern to begin the program. After the requisite formalities of welcome and expressions of gratitude to the administration, no members of which, he noted to himself, were yet in attendance, he began the speech on which he had labored for weeks.

"Forty years ago," Matthews began, "Ralph Waldo Emerson called America 'the country of the Future . . . a country of beginnings . . . and expectations.' Yet in that same year, he also wrote the following: 'Our culture is very cheap and intelligible. Unroof any house, and you shall find it. The well-being consists in having a sufficiency of coffee and toast, with a daily newspaper; a well-glazed parlor, with marbles, mirrors, and centre-table; and the excitement of a few parties and a few rides in a year.' America, he said, 'has not fulfilled what seemed the reasonable expectation of mankind.'

"These words are more true today than when Emerson wrote them. Hundreds of thousands of Americans have lost their lives fighting, surely, for something more than this. America is built not of bricks and iron but of ideals, vision, and hope. And a foundational stated belief in the possibilities of mankind.

"Freedom is the very oxygen of those possibilities. This has been the axiom through a century, and more, of struggle. These states paid in blood for independence from England—not once but twice—and we have paid in blood again, less than twenty years ago, not only to emancipate the enslaved Negro but to earn the nation the opportunity to rededicate itself—on a more durable footing—to its stated ideals. One would think it obvious that the shaping of that freedom, and the sharpening of the sense of responsibility that must go along with it, would require not only the good will but the constant attention, and earnest hard work, of all our citizens.

"Yet after all the suffering, and all the work, where do we find ourselves? America too often takes that freedom for granted, regarding it only as an entitlement to enrich oneself to the greatest possible degree—and, failing that, to be left alone with one's complacency and Emerson's 'coffee and toast, newspaper, and well-glazed parlor.' Our nation is in trouble. The voices of imagination and moral force have been drowned out by the babble of the marketplace. The truth itself is mocked as if it were delusion, and our Constitution treated as an inconvenience, rather than as the sacred contract that it is. Words are twisted to mean their opposites and our ideals traded for cheap advantage.

"This week-end's conference is an unprecedented event, a conversation about America's future, the role of literature in that future, and the nature of freedom itself. It is my hope—our hope—that this conversation may shine light on a way forward for our country. I would like to dedicate these proceedings to the memory of Ralph Waldo Emerson. Joining me on the dais this morning are two of our greatest writers; I have asked them to begin their remarks by reading a passage of their own selection from their respective works, and I have asked Walt Whitman to begin." Applause, and he returned to his seat at the dais.

The poet stood slowly, removing his hat and setting it down at his place on the dais, where it loomed between Matthews and

Melville like a fourth participant in the panel. At the lectern, Whitman took his time opening a copy of *Leaves of Grass*, which he had borrowed from one of the lobby tables, and paging through it to find his desired passage. Then, the page located, he bellowed,

"I AM OF OLD AND YOUNG . . ."

Almost as one, the audience emitted a gasp, hearing not the modulated cadences one might have expected from a poet but the full-throated bray of a roustabout:

> . . . of the foolish as much as the wise,
> Regardless of others, ever regardful of others,
> Maternal as well as paternal, a child as well as a man,
> A Southerner soon as a Northerner, a planter nonchalant and
>   hospitable down by the Oconee I live,
> A Yankee bound my own way ready for trade, my joints the
>   limberest joints on earth and the sternest joints on earth,
> A Kentuckian walking the vale of the Elkhorn in my deer-skin
>   leggings, a Louisianian or Georgian,
> A boatman over lakes or bays or along coasts, a Hoosier, Badger,
>   Buck-eye. . . .

The lines rolled out as if pounding through ocean swells, proclaiming limitless vistas, and the listeners seemed to brace themselves against the backs of their seats with every new proclamation:

> Of every hue and cast am I, of every rank and religion,
> A farmer, mechanic, artist, gentleman, sailor, Quaker,
> Prisoner, fancy-man, rowdy, lawyer, physician, priest.
> I resist anything better than my own diversity.

With those words, Whitman shut the copy of *Leaves of Grass* with a loud clap; after a brief moment the audience applauded vigorously and shouted its approval. Whitman waited until it subsided, then he began his remarks.

"We're supposed to be talking this morning about literature and America," he said. "I never made the distinction. America is a large country, a country of the body as well as the mind. It's a country of distance, so it's a country of movement. The question is what holds it together. Our host mentioned Emerson. I knew him. He had a big effect on me when I was young, like he did on a lot of people. I didn't think he was much of a poet. What he said boiled down to two things: 'Nature is the greatest classroom,' and 'God is to be found in each individual, within.' There's a lot of foam on top, but that's the beer. Bottom up, not top down. There you have the foundation of it.

"I'm getting old, but I still live in the material world. Fields and rivers, mountains, plains, birds . . . Those are our true Constitution. We are done with Europe; America is the land of the new man, and the new woman. But where is the American *literature* equal to our bridges and our railroads? Or our steamboats and factories? Where is a poem equal to a well-made table? Or a novel worthy of the trees cut down to produce its paper? We want a literature of cobblers at their benches, women giving birth, leather workers, riverboat men, cotton farmers, cities, buses, and trains. . . . Instead we get imitations of European parlor farces, preening sentences, stale perfume, social envy, gossip, petty ambition, timid men with digestive problems."

A few titters swept the hall. These encouraged him to continue in this vein, railing against "desiccated romances and writers unequal to, and afraid of, the proportions of the nation." He ended his remarks by saying, "Of all writers, I have come closest to singing America's possibility. But one writer is not a literature—not even me!"

There was laughter at the cheekiness of the assertion, and the ensuing applause was loud enough that no one but Frederick Matthews heard Herman Melville exclaim, "*Good God. . . .*"

Whitman returned to the dais, where he replaced his hat upon his head and enjoyed the applause, smiling and waving. It took a while for the hall to quiet. Matthews then introduced Melville, who made his way to the lectern carrying the book he had brought with him and staring at the floor.

On Friday morning I found myself slouched in the third row of Midlake Auditorium, still smarting from the rude rejection I had received at the door of the previous night's "welcome party," and listening to Walt Whitman and Herman Melville drone on about this and that. I was suffering as well from the considerable after-effects of my subsequent visit to the Echo Tavern.

Early the previous afternoon, a cable had arrived from the New York *World*.

> Send report writer confab stop if interesting will run stop regards to Twain from Tilley stop

I had all but danced a jig as I read it for a third, then a fourth, time. They were inviting me to submit a notice about the week-end's events. And to deliver greetings to Mark Twain from "Tilley"— no doubt a lady admirer. "*If interesting will run.*" Of course! No reporter ever earned a name filing stories headlined *CALM SEA OFF NANTUCKET.* I resolved to make the most of this.

I readied myself to attend the party that had been arranged for the just-arrived participants, the Institute faculty, and the Satraps and Pashas of the city's business community. With the *World*'s imprimatur, I expected to be welcomed warmly despite the fact that admission was by invitation only and I had not been invited.

Around 6:30 p.m. I entered the grounds of the Auburn Collegiate Institute and made my way to Founders' Hall, where I attempted to join the parade of dignitaries as they filed in. But a formidable presence at the entryway, a veritable Amazon in a rough grey gown that appeared to be sewn from burlap, informed me that the party was only for the participants, faculty, et c.

"I am a member of the press," I said, "writing a story for the New York *World*."

"I wasn't informed," she said, turning to greet Amos Smith, the president of the Cayuga Savings Bank, and his wife, as they entered.

"An oversight, I'm sure," I said. "I will find Professor Matthews and he will correct the situation. Excuse me," I said, and took a step toward the ballroom door, but was blocked by a prodigious arm belonging to the aforementioned Amazon.

"Don't try that again," she said. "This is a private function. You speak English?"

"Ah," I said. "I understand completely. That, by the way, is a lovely dress you are wearing."

"Get out of here," she said, and I do believe she would have enforced the directive personally. I lingered outside for a bit, but I could not bring myself to be the character lurking in the shadows, collaring the quality as they made their entrances. The party was not important to my article, I told myself; the main event would commence in the morning. I was more than a little irritated, none-theless, at being barred, and I repaired to the Echo, as mentioned.

Now it was Friday morning. Outside, the air was fresh and the sky clear; I cannot pretend that I found myself interested in the words from the stage, and in fact the headache that I had brought with me seemed to swell with each new pronouncement. Half-way through Whitman's reading of some horrible "poem," I rose from my seat as unobtrusively as I could and stepped out into the lobby, which turned out to be nearly as well populated as the auditorium.

A small mob had coagulated in the bookselling area, where

a gentleman resembling an undernourished heron ran back and forth behind the book tables, attending to customers. I heard a woman's voice saying, "*Edward Goodheart*? Oh, I think you may see him again." Pushing my way in to get a glimpse, I saw that the voice belonged to a woman who could only have been Lucy Comstock, seated behind a small mountain of books, holding forth for a crowd of customers as the heron accepted the money thrust at him by those eager to gain a signed book as a relic of their audience with greatness.

I joined the mob as she was greeted by a babble of fresh questions about various personages in her books, all of which she answered while deploying an arsenal of coquettish winks, meaningful glances, and tinkling laughter and at the same time looking down at whatever book was offered for the next signature, asking the petitioner's name, inscribing the book even as she answered another question from someone in the crowd with, in each instance, some turn or fillip of wit or flirtation. All in all she was very impressive and, one felt, not someone whose displeasure one would wish to risk.

After a while, as the swarm around Miss Comstock showed no signs of dispersing, I peeled myself away. I noticed a solitary young woman at the far end of the tables, reading one of the displayed volumes, peacefully enough, as if Lucy Comstock and her disciples were several continents away. I thought it might be worthwhile to have the voices of a few paying attendees in the article, and I assumed that she was one. And she was, I will admit, rather attractive, with dark red hair pulled back severely from her brow, certainly not a reason to avoid a conversation, I thought. As I approached I saw that she was perusing *Leaves of Grass*. I had my notebook out and I introduced myself, told her that I was a reporter writing an article about the conference.

Her eyes remained on the page she was reading.

"Have you read Whitman before?" I asked.

"I am reading him now," she replied, her eyes still on the page.

"Do you like the poems?"

"There is quite a lot of wind blowing these leaves around," she said. Then she closed the book and made an abrupt departure. What an odd one, I thought; nervous as a hummingbird.

I spent a few more minutes hovering around before I saw Mark Twain enter the reception area, accompanied by Forrest Taylor. I recognized Taylor because I had seen him announce himself to the Amazon outside the welcome party the night before. His boots alone might have earned him a citation for valor. He and Twain were apparently sharing a joke. I started toward them as Taylor took his leave and walked off down a hallway.

I introduced myself to Twain as a fellow newsman, and he shook my hand while drawing on a cigar and taking a quick, sharp inventory of my face. I asked him if he had been acquainted with General Taylor before the conference, and he said he hadn't, and that they had only just met.

"He's a son of a bitch," Twain said, "but he tells a good story."

"Are you speaking after lunch?"

"That's the idea," he said, looking around distractedly. "Have you seen the Master of the Revels anywhere? I have a couple boxes of books that require disposition."

"Do you mean Matthews? The organizer?"

"Matthews, yes," he said.

"He's inside the auditorium conducting the conversation between Melville and Whitman."

"Really?" he said, looking at me now. "I should have liked to see that."

"It was something of a soporific, I'm afraid," I said.

Now his features tightened slightly, although he continued to display a smile that was no longer that of the collegial fellow journalist I'd expected. "Writing books isn't easy," he said. "Those two are great writers. Don't you think so?"

"Oh, of course," I said. "I meant that they had been assigned a ponderous topic—Emerson, the future of America, the nature of freedom. . . ."

He was regarding me now with a purely professional smile, and eyes that had clearly come to a decision as to the degree to which I was to be taken seriously. He clapped me on the shoulder with one hand, said, "See you later," and walked off in the direction of the book sales, where a number of acolytes had already noted his presence and were standing ready to greet him.

I did not have time to brood on what seemed to have been a conversational *faux pas* with Twain, as I heard angry shouting from within the auditorium. I cursed myself for missing a moment when something might actually have happened, and I started for the doors to the auditorium just as they flew open and a small flood of attendees emerged.

During Whitman's presentation, Melville had grown gloomy. His mood of the night before had lifted earlier, but now it clouded over again. Whitman's blithe-sounding assertions of unbounded entitlement had grated on him. Whitman's lines spread in every direction, honey from a broken jar, a vision, as Melville heard it, of life without consequences. Not to mention the clear implication that Whitman was the sole worthwhile writer yet produced in America. This, in a program to feature Twain, Frederick Douglass—himself, for the love of God . . .

At the lectern now, Melville trudged through a meandering

description of *Clarel*, during which he felt the audience growing restless, and then he began reading a lengthy excerpt:

> Hypothesise,
> If be a people which began
> Without impediment, or let
> From any ruling which foreran;
> Even striving all things to forget
> But this—the excellence of man
> Left to himself, his natural bent,
> His own devices and intent;
> And if, in satire of the heaven,
> A world, a new world have been given
> For stage whereon to deploy the event;
> If such a people be—well, well,
> One hears the kettledrums of hell!

Several dozen lines later, he finished to scattered applause and took some moments before beginning his remarks with an apology.

"I am afraid," he began, "that my words may have sounded too pessimistic after Mr. Whitman's reading. The vision of the fresh start begins many great adventures. But that vision also begins many tales of punished pride. We face the rising sun of possibility, but we disregard the long shadows it casts behind us.

"I hear much of Emerson in Mr. Whitman's vision of America's shining prospects, and the sound almost of a wounded lover in his disappointment at America's failure to live up to his expectations. Emerson often seemed blind to the dark side of human possibility. His imagination of the universal efficacy of good-will and frankness was, in my view, naïve, despite his undeniable energy and intelligence. There has never been, nor will there ever be, a 'new man'—only new ways of stating the same age-old agonies."

During these words, Whitman's attention was focused on the table in front of him, where his hands were performing some detailed activity as he emitted various faint, guttural groans. Those in the first rows saw that he was folding a small sheet of paper into the shape of a bird. When he began manipulating the paper bird as if it were walking along the surface of the table they chuckled audibly.

Melville stopped talking for a moment and directed his gaze at Whitman. If Whitman noticed, he gave no sign. When Melville resumed, his voice was sharper.

"And I hear Emerson also in Whitman's Homeric catalogues of human types—all the 'planters' and 'traders' and 'Kentuckians,' and 'Georgians,' and 'prisoners' and 'priests.' Human souls do not represent such easy categories. Missing from these lists are complex *individuals*. No one is defined by these labels. One is marked by one's geographical beginnings, or one's chosen occupation, or the color of one's skin, or one's religious beliefs, but no one is *defined* by these, except in the minds of those who would use them for some ulterior purpose, who would turn men into machine parts. . . ."

At these words, Whitman grumbled audibly, "I do not wish men to be machine parts."

"And, too," Melville went on, "if in good faith one imagines the playing out of that vision, those constituent 'parts' will come to insist upon the aspects that distinguish them, which insistence will lead inevitably to the sharpest disagreements among the 'parts.' What of those whose good will has been eroded or subverted—whose cause has been left behind? What of the Southern Negro who finds himself all but re-enslaved despite the promise of emancipation? What of the Southern planter who finds himself suddenly without free labor? What of the factory owner who is told that he must pay his workers higher wages? And then what of the demagogue, waiting to inflame the sense of grievance among these parties? Self-interest, the prejudices of the uneducated, the cynicism of the over-educated, the anger of the abused, the monomania of the leader intoxicated by power . . . These cannot be wished away by your generalities or hopes."

During this oration Whitman had grown visibly agitated. Finally he shouted, "You are distorting my meaning."

"Am I?" Melville said. "I am sorry for it, then. But did you not say that you consider your poetry the only worthwhile literature produced in America?"

"When have I said that?"

"Does Mark Twain write 'drawing room comedies,' or whatever your phrase was? Or Mrs. Stowe? Or myself, for that matter . . ."

"I will admit that I don't write interminable stories about shipwrecks," Whitman said. "I don't write poems about the end of the human race, narrated by little puppets: this one's idea, that one's idea. . . . I stand on my own feet! I sing myself!"

"You sing nothing else!" Melville responded.

Whitman pushed back his chair and stood up.

Matthews, clearly alarmed, pushed back his own chair and cried, "Please!" The audience was confused—expressions of consternation erupted, shouted questions, catcalls.

Melville quit the lectern and made for the stage steps.

Matthews hurriedly announced that the panel would adjourn for lunch and return at two p.m.—valiantly adding that the afternoon discussion, on "The Writer's Life," would feature Mark Twain, Lucy Comstock, and . . . The names of the others were lost in the hubbub as the lobby doors opened. "Please browse the book tables outside," he shouted.

He turned to Whitman and saw on the poet's face an expression of simple happiness, placid and serene, as if he had been awakened from a pleasant nap.

"Are you all right?" Matthews said, to Whitman. Melville had opened one of the lobby doors and was leaving the hall.

"Of course," Whitman said. "Are we to take lunch now?"

Matthews replied in the affirmative, then he ran off to the edge of the stage and down the steps in pursuit of Melville.

As the crowd spilled out around me into the lobby I was nearly knocked off my feet by Lecturer Matthews, who emerged looking around with a stricken aspect. Without greeting me directly, he said, "Have you seen Melville?"

"Wasn't he sharing a stage with you?" I asked.

"Weren't you inside for the presentation?"

"Well, yes," I said, in partial truth. "Yes, I was. First-class, I'd say."

"I thought I saw you leave midway through," he said, his eyes searching the lobby. The fellow was not quite as straightforward as I had taken him to be.

"I had just come out to visit the Men's," I said, "if you must know, and I . . ."

Before I could get the sentence out he looked over my shoulder, swiveled on his heel, and all but ran away from me.

I do not enjoy being treated as disposable. I turned, curious to see what might have precipitated this rudeness, and saw a local character who could often be encountered on Auburn street corners collaring passersby. I had always taken him for a Negro, although he might well have been an Iroquois, or even a well-tanned descendant of Abraham. On this morning he was wearing a turban with some kind of brooch set in the middle of it, resembling a blood-shot eye. Well, I thought, perhaps he will be able to tell me what just transpired. I approached and greeted him.

"The Prophet will be heard," he said, following Matthews with his eyes as the lecturer quit the lobby for the great outdoors.

"Yes," I said, smelling something potentially useful on the breeze. "Yes, he will." I asked if he had attended the morning's presentation.

He looked me straight in the eye. "The oceans will conceal their spawn until the salt dries upon the coral."

He was silent, holding my gaze as if I might have the correct response. All right, I thought, I will see that, and raise you. "The cave is silent," I replied, "until the echo is heard."

At this his eyes grew wide. "Why was I not allowed to speak?" he said.

Ah, I thought. Why, indeed. "Yes," I said, testing the water, "I had hoped to hear you."

As if I had removed the finger from the storied dike, a torrent was loosed; he emitted a fantastical tirade, which I tried to capture, but it was really quite useless, scraps of Biblical cadence colliding with references to classical antiquity, here a few shreds of Ezekiel, cohabiting with Habakkuk; there a reference to Plato's cave, the Bhagavad Gita, the Book of Isaiah, mixed up with the Declaration of Independence . . . such a flow should be harnessed, I thought to myself.

". . . and I was a lamentation unto the multitude," he was saying, "even unto the generations. In the course of events we count the lilies of the field, founding upon this continent the better angels of judgment. And such judgment shall not perish until Leviathan meet with stern rebuke!"

This seemed to be a stopping point for him. Feeling the tongue of inspiration tickling me, I told him that I was looking forward to his presentation at the conference. "Will it be later this afternoon?" I asked, innocently.

"I am not on the schedule," he said. "He would not let me prophesize."

"Well, then," I began, "you should make room for yourself. Go in there after lunch and make yourself heard! Doesn't Scripture say that wisdom is better than rubies, and the lips of the righteous feed many?" It said something along those lines, I was almost certain.

He seemed lost in a private cave of thought. "Maybe," he said. "I can't do it this afternoon." He seemed about to say something, then he walked off without another word.

Evidently the morning session had ended most abruptly, and the attendees were off to some midday recreation. I made a few inquiries and learned that the two literary eminences had come near to fisticuffs onstage, and that the conference was to resume in the mid-afternoon with a panel on "The Writer's Life," which was to include most of the participants involved. I hoped that some of the interested parties I had encountered in Town Line might by then have found their way to Mount Parnassus. In the meantime I stepped outside into the lovely morning air, where I was immediately accosted by three ladies, whom I did not at first recognize.

"There you are!" one of them said. "We were delayed on the road. Has the conference begun?"

"It has," I responded, still not sure who they were, "but I am afraid you have missed the morning session. Apparently there was some disturbance, and they have broken for lunch."

"Well, we are ready for them when they resume," the leader said, and I realized right then that these were some of the suffragists whom I had encountered in Seneca Falls.

"Not a word, so far," I said, "about women's suffrage. Shameful."

"Shameful, but no surprise," this woman said. "I shall look forward to their reaction when we hold them to account."

"As shall I," I said, with true sincerity. Things were looking up. The leader headed for the lobby entrance with one of her companions, while the third, lagging back slightly, asked in a low voice whether Lucy Comstock had yet made an appearance.

"Why, yes," I said. "She is entertaining an audience inside the lobby. You will see."

Her face brightened and she all but exclaimed before she remembered to compose herself and direct a complicitous look in my direction. She followed her compatriots inside, and I left Midlake in search of something to eat. I wanted to be well fortified for the afternoon's festivities.

—6—

"SEE WITH YOUR OWN EYES! Speak with your own tongue! Discover the land for yourself! Plant your flag and declare yourself king—or queen!—of all you discover! Join hands with the thief as well as the minister! Be healthful and free, a friend to your sisters as well as your brothers. . . ."

Forrest Taylor, late CSA, sat alone at lunch in Founders' Hall, listening to the thundering hooves of Whitman's rhetoric, three tables away, stampeding through the impressionable minds of four young acolytes. How different the world looked to the victors and to the subjugated, he thought. How entitled they feel. How easy to slouch in a dirty coat and a velvet cravat, idling at the docks with other sodomites while men trained to the most severe discipline fought and died for honor and loyalty.

He had learned that his only appearance during this week-end was to take place the following day on a stage which he would share with Frederick Douglass. The equivalent, under the geographical and historical circumstances, to being issued a mule and a butter knife and sent into action against a brigade of mounted cavalry. And a grand total of two copies of his own book displayed at the bookseller's table, surrounded by mountains of Douglass and Twain and Comstock to balm the affronted complacencies. Twain, at least, saw both sides, or he acted as if he did. He, Forrest Taylor, believed that he saw both sides as well. Saw both, and hated one with a passion that would never exhaust itself.

Why, exactly, had he made this trip? He was quite certain he must have had a reason. . . . His late father, himself a hero of the Mexican War, had once told him that nothing good ever came of spite. If such were indeed the case, and Taylor had no doubt that it was, then he was getting the proper repayment for his likely motive.

Seething. His wife, sick at home, her feet and hands turning inexorably into claws, had been cruelly condemned first to canes, which became useless, then a wheel-chair, then a bed, where she required constant attention from a detachment of nurses. Why should she, who was without blame, have this debilitating condition? She, who danced gracefully at cotillion, now with her feet turned inward like an owl's, and her face disfigured by pain. He would demand an accounting of a God who would let this happen to the flower of his life, while beasts in human form were allowed to roam free with impunity, strutting in clothes that would be laughable on a white man. Furious with the injustice of it . . .

What barbarities, he thought, in the name of a democracy for which the beneficiaries could not trace the etymology nor grasp the cost. The laws of Solon and Pericles replaced by the children's fables of an Ethiopian slave, while the storehouse was robbed to the foundation. And the self-righteous crowing of the self-anointed pioneers of universal freedom and suffrage, as if the entire scaffolding of civilization had not from the beginning depended upon the labor of enslaved men. When have the conquered not been enslaved, he thought? As if the Christianity they cite as their justification for the rape of the Southern states were not, itself, enriched by power and domination. We subdued the land, made it yield unimaginable prosperity, until the conquerors from the North said, "Thank you very much, we will now relieve you of the benefits of the work you have done. And our lieutenants—illiterate savages—will be your schoolmasters, your legislators, and your daughters' husbands." Making possible this fatuous "freedom," and for whom? Free to do what? In the name of what? He would do as much damage as he could, here, before they rang the curtain down. . . .

———————

> Thorns have roses—panoply,
> Viceroy of assent
> Who could guess—the secret dagger—
> Pointed intent

She wrote the lines even as she recognized their fatal imperfections. "Secret dagger" advertised an unwelcome melodramatic posture. "Viceroy" was inexact, as well. The idea was well enough, the inversion of the roles, not the danger guarding the fragile prize but instead the fragrant prize masking a malevolence . . . but the third and fourth lines might have been purloined from an opera— Sicilian revenge—or the Orient!

> Thorns have roses—
> Panoply of assent

Better.

> Perfume—camouflage
> Of pointed intent

From the other end of the room echoed Whitman's imperial cadences. She had earlier taken her leave of an unpleasant young man at the book tables and gone to the auditorium, where Whitman and Melville were inciting one another to a terrible shouting. The few minutes she'd spent in reading through Whitman's book did nothing to dispel her negative impression of his abilities and intentions. Mr. Higginson had written that it was "no discredit" to Whitman that he wrote *Leaves of Grass*, "only that he did not burn it afterward," which she thought an overstep, yet the remark was adhesive, and it had affixed itself to her idea of the book. Even its removal would have left its mark.

She looked up from her notebook; a beautiful late morning could be seen outside the great windows, and she thought of the young man onstage, at the panel's helm. He had kindled some recognition in her, and a heightened attention. The unruly lock of hair was a poignancy. Was there a kinship of spirit? Suddenly across the sky, turning, like an ice-skater, a hawk, glorious, and she thought of Hopkins's lines, the heel sweeping smooth. . . . She would have summoned Donne to the dais for the afternoon session. Was the nation nothing but a fraying quilt of livid prose urgencies, a land too coarse for poetry? O, that she might invoke a river and skate upon it, trace a figure that angels could admire. . . . There had been word of a circus set up on the town's outskirts; a poster bore the news. An elephant, and spangled riders. Would she own the wherewithal to emerge and grasp? Or only sing the passing-by?

How are you enjoying your roasted beef, Mrs. Stowe? It is fine, Mrs. Stowe—the greatest culinary event in the history of the world. Unfortunately she was missing the sword that ought to have been provided in order to slice it. Maybe the stew would have been edible. Twain had told her to meet him there at the luncheon, but of course there was no sign of him. Only Whitman gassing at the end of the dining room; she had sat as far away as possible. The girl writing in the notebook looked vaguely familiar.

Mrs. Stowe had raked along the book tables for a while before coming to Founders' Hall. The bookseller had her two most recent, and a tall stack of *Uncle Tom*, pirated by some thief in Philadelphia. She had insisted that the seller remove the copies immediately, but only after she had made note of the "publisher's" name and location. After turning away, she thought better, turned back, and ordered the hapless man to give her one of the unauthorized copies—"for evidence," she said, but the fact was that she had initiated a private vice, several years back, of collecting the bootlegged issues and displaying them proudly in her library, along with any printed examples of the hideously disfigured "dramatic" versions. She derived a perverse satisfaction at seeing the spines arrayed along her shelves.

She was to take part in a "panel" beginning at two p.m. She considered feigning her own death in order to avoid discoursing upon the assigned topic, "the life of the writer," but of course she would not; she would participate, what was left of her working brain would congeal, but at least the company would be good on the dais. Frederick Douglass—rarefied air. Although also the perfumed inanities sure to emerge from Lucy Comstock, whom she had met once in Northampton. She had not yet got the taste out of her mouth, and that was two years previous.

And where was Twain, anyway?

Sparse crowds along the hay-strewn midway. He strolled unnoticed, past the wooden livestock stalls, the pitch-and-toss booths with the bored-looking boys sitting in front, waiting for somebody with a girlfriend and a throwing arm, three balls for a penny, the stuffed dolls and gewgaws. He had spent half an hour signing books and dispensing handshakes in the lobby of Midlake Hall, until the clamorous attendees had mostly gone off to the lunch, then back at Harmony House he donned a plain, rough jacket, buttoned his shirt at the neck, pulled a beat-up hat down as far as he could, awakened the slumbering driver in his barouche behind the house, and, giving him the necessary directions, settled back in the seat for a five-minute ride. He could have easily walked it, but he did not want to chance missing the afternoon presentation, in which he was supposed to be the featured speaker.

It was a small carnival, as they went, like the traveling menageries he saw as a boy, and it brought him back to a time he would revisit at any opportunity. The Hawaiian leg show behind the painted plywood front, a line of "Scottish" dancers, a man with an accordion. There were the Romany fortune-tellers, and a lady weight lifter. And there, at the end of the midway, the little platform from which two men he knew were enjoying an intermission.

"Hello, Charlie," Twain said.

"Hello, Sam," the other man said, putting his cigar into his mouth and sticking out his hand for a shake. "What are you doing here?"

"Delivering my eternal wisdom at a college up the road. I expect to be canonized next month."

"Henry's in back."

"I thought as much. Is he accepting visitors?"

"Toss a bucket on him first to wake him up. You wanting to borrow him again?"

"Let me see what kind of shape he's in."

Mark Twain pulled the makeshift curtain to one side and, stepping into the area reserved for performers—not much more than a badly tended barn stall—placed a foot squarely into a pile of manure—horse, from the smell and consistency.

"Goddamnation," he growled, which woke up his old friend, who was asleep on some rough wooden crates.

"Mister Sam!" the reclining figure said. "I told Charlie we should clean that mess up or either put up a sign."

"Nothing some kerosene won't take care of," Twain said, scraping what he could onto the side of some stacked-up wood. "How have you been? You keeping up your Shakespeare?"

The man called Henry chuckled at the question as he righted himself and stood up slowly from his makeshift bed. Twain had done the best he could with his shoe, and the two men shook hands.

"Can I borrow you this afternoon for half an hour or so?"

"Ask Mister Charlie. It's fine with me."

"He'll say yes; I'll make up for any lost receipts. You look like you lost some weight."

"Shoot," Henry said. "You want songs, or a recitation, or . . ."

"I figured songs and whatever else comes to mind. I'm betting the place can use some livening up."

"You betting with me?"

"I'm no fool, Henry," Twain said. The two men laughed and Twain clapped Henry on the shoulder.

"Miss 'Livia doing okay?" Henry said.

"Yes, thank you, and the girls are fine. I'll tell them you asked after them. I think New Haven was the last time they saw you?"

Henry shook his head. "Naw—Providence. You all were up there for something."

"I'll send the carriage down for you around two. That be okay?"

"Sure."

"Throw them a couple of curves."

"Undoubtedly," Henry said. "It would be anathema to me to present even the briefest program of unalloyed buffoonery."

"That's the stuff," Twain said, laughing. "You're a genius, Henry. Glad you don't write books; I'd have to have you hijacked and taken away someplace."

"Wouldn't be the first time, Mister Sam. Old Henry's been 'buked and scorned, hijacked too."

"See you in a while," Twain said, carefully avoiding the pile of manure as he pulled the curtain aside and stepped outside to arrange things with his friend Charlie.

"Are you all right?"

The young host, standing silhouetted against the glowing green morning lawn. Himself seated under a tree.

"Yes," Herman Melville replied. "Thank you." After a moment, he added, "I am sorry for my part in that melodrama, inside. Perhaps it was a farce. In any case . . ."

"Will you come and take lunch?"

"No," Melville said. "I must return home."

Alarm on the young man's face.

"But you are to be on the afternoon panel."

"Everything I might add is already in my books. I am an empty purse."

"Please," the young man, Matthews, was saying. "This conference will not be complete without your participation."

"What can I do?" Melville said. The birds, the strollers, the crisp sunshine amid the starched elm leaves.

"Join the afternoon discussion. Please. And if you must leave afterward I will make the arrangements, although I hope you will stay for tomorrow as well. Frederick Douglass admires you greatly."

Remembered what he said about *Benito*.

"What *should* I do?" Melville said. "I mean where should I go until it is time for the panel?"

"I would be honored to escort you to lunch. Or if you would prefer to rest at Harmony House . . ."

Groups of people at table, squalls of attention or its opposite, the meal interrupted. But back in the room—as well place one's head in a nest of yellow-jackets . . .

"Perhaps I will walk around town a bit," he said. "That might settle my mood somewhat."

"Well . . ."

"If there is a public-house where I might eat something simple and collect my thoughts for the afternoon."

"Of course. The session begins at two, but you should have more than enough time."

"Good." Melville stood up, still limber for his years. "I will return refreshed. . . ."

"I found your poem very interesting," Matthews said. "The idea that there might be something inherently destined to pull apart in the democracy . . ."

Grabbed by the ankle while making his exit . . . Ungar's words, not his . . . he looked up at the cloudless blue and inhaled deeply.

"Thank you," Melville said. "Thank you, truly. I will see you at two p.m." And he walked away before that floating moment could be reeled in and bound fast to his listing ship.

— 7 —

I MADE MY WAY TO Holyfield Hall after the conversation with Melville, hoping to spend some minutes alone in my office collecting myself. Upon entering the foyer I all but collided with Miss Pound, from the English Department office, who informed me that her friend Juliette, who had volunteered to sell admission tickets at the doorway, had not shown up, and a goodly number of unregistered attendees had apparently been admitted.

I had not noticed this, nor had I thought to check when I arrived that morning, so preoccupied had I been with my opening talk and the prospect of sharing a stage with Melville and Whitman. I asked Miss Pound if it were possible to find a replacement, and she replied that her sister would be available for the next afternoon's session, but not before. This meant that the session about to begin would also be open at no charge. This was disturbing news, for obvious reasons, but there was nothing to be done about it at that moment.

I thanked her for letting me know and started toward my office again, but I was intercepted by Wickham Moreland's secretary, who informed me that the provost had received a report of the unpleasantness at the early session and wanted to speak with me.

"Now?" I said.

"Yes."

She led me into Moreland's chamber, where I found myself, once again, facing Wickham Moreland across his desk. This time, he did not gesture for me to sit down.

"Are these men alcoholics?" he said, with no preamble.

"Sir?"

"Will the entire conference continue in this vein? Have you had an explanation? People storming off the stage . . . What is this about?"

"Ah," I said, trying to think quickly while smiling reassuringly. "Yes. Of course. All is well, but Mr. Melville had received some sad news just before the program. By telegram, from his wife, and he was very upset. His horse had to be shot, I'm afraid. Broken leg, and it was his favorite . . ."

This was, of course, conceivably the most ridiculous excuse I had yet offered for anything in my adult life. And what in God's name would I do if Moreland encountered Melville later and offered his condolences? What was I thinking? Moreland was watching me, squinting slightly, as if trying to read a page of newsprint through a layer of gauze. I thought I might even have seen a slight wince of sympathy—for the horse, no doubt.

"He said that he would put it out of his mind," I went on, "for the remainder of the conference. And he asked me to tell no one, as he was afraid that any expression of sympathy would set him off again. He was quite embarrassed."

"His horse," Moreland said. "I suppose I could understand. But still . . ."

As I watched him I noticed something I had not realized before. He, too, was in unfamiliar territory. He had something to lose, and he was worried. We had a shared interest in the success of the conference, albeit for different reasons. Of course. This gave me some confidence, and I continued by saying, "The afternoon panel gives every promise of being a triumph," in my heartiest voice.

"This will feature Mark Twain?" he said.

"Yes!" I said. "He is the featured speaker, along with Miss Comstock, Mrs. Stowe, and Frederick Douglass. . . ."

"Understand," he said, "I will be bringing Amos Smith to the afternoon session tomorrow, from the Cayuga Bank, along with Mrs. Smith, Mr. Howard from Seneca Trust, and Mr. Littlefield from Canandaigua Bank. If their impression is of some sort of circus or anarchist revival meeting, this will redound very unpleasantly to the reputation of the Institute, as well as to myself, both personally and professionally, and, I cannot emphasize strongly enough, to you and your own career. Much effort and many resources have been rallied in support of this experiment."

"I can assure you," I said, "that Mr. Twain and Miss Comstock will provide excellent . . . entertainment."

"Good," he said. "Make certain of it." Then he seemed to remember something and asked, "Are the receipts satisfactory? I hear that the hall was less than full."

"Receipts!" I said. "Of course! I have not had a moment's opportunity to check, but at the last tally we appeared to be in very good shape."

"What is the dollar figure?"

"Yes," I said. "It is slipping my mind, but I will get that for you."

I left his chambers somewhat shaken, to say the least. I barely had time to close my own office door, sit at my desk, and bow my head for a long moment before I needed to leave once again and take up the reins at Midlake.

Upon returning to Midlake I had just noted the empty admission table sitting as if in silent reproach, when I heard a loud, matter-of-fact woman's voice say, "Are you Matthews?"

I turned in the direction of this voice to find four women standing in a line, staring at me. I replied that I was Lecturer Matthews and asked, "With whom do I have the pleasure of speaking?"

My interlocutor introduced herself as Mrs. Margaret Lewis

Stanford, and I felt my viscera attempting to flee the scene without me. The name belonged to a notorious firebrand who had been one of the organizers of the famous Seneca Falls conference years before, a close associate of Susan B. Anthony's in the struggle for women's rights. In person, her aspect was truly daunting, and that of her companions hardly less so.

"Ah! Greetings, greetings!" I said, bowing to Mrs. Stanford and then making a general bow to the other ladies. One of them nodded coolly in response to my bow; the others did not. "I am so pleased that you have come!"

Mrs. Stanford ignored my proffered hand. "Why is there no session in your program dedicated to the fight for women's suffrage?"

The bluntness of the question somewhat stunned me, especially as I had not a hint of a ready reply. It was of course one of the principal topics of the time, yet I had not thought to invite a specialist in the area. I stammered some words of apology, implying that attempts had been made and I had been unable to find an adequate spokeswoman. . . .

"I heard nothing of any such attempt," she replied. "It doesn't matter in any event. We are here to ensure that the issue is addressed."

"And I am so glad you are," I replied. "Thank you for making the effort to travel such a distance. I know that your presence will lend both brilliance and gravity to the—"

"Please stop," she said. "An excess of sugar gives me cramps." And with that she led her troops into the auditorium.

Within the half-hour, all the participants except Mark Twain were assembled on the stage. We had added a second table to accommodate everyone. Melville had shown up in a much improved mood.

His aspect was so benevolent—he greeted me with a broad smile and the word "Ahoy!"—that I dismissed any worry over a revisiting of the morning's hostilities. I did wonder if he might have found his way to a tavern since I'd seen him; his face was flushed. Mrs. Stowe occupied a chair next to the empty one reserved for Twain, her face expressing a mild general disapproval. Seated to her left, Whitman seemed in a muted mood, perhaps contrite for his morning outburst. Lucy Comstock had moved her own chair as far away from Whitman as possible and sat conversing cordially with Frederick Douglass.

The hall was filling nearly to capacity. Mrs. Stanford's group had occupied the center of the audience, eight rows back. In the front rows were Wickham Moreland, Chairman Olander alongside a woman whom I assumed was his wife, and several civic grandees who had attended the previous night's welcome party. Forrest Taylor, who was not scheduled to participate in the program until the next day, had installed himself in the hall's second row, wearing an inscrutable smile that I could not call agreeable. Not far from him I noted the reporter who had interviewed me and, that morning, collared me in the lobby when I went looking for Melville. I did not trust that fellow.

It was nearing the two o'clock hour when I noticed Twain standing just outside the auditorium doors, beckoning me to the lobby. Praying that there would not be another disaster added to the day's list, I rose from my seat, descended the steps from the stage, and joined Twain outside the doors. There I found that he had a companion with him, a Negro with light, almost copper-colored skin, green eyes, and grey-flecked hair, who was holding a banjo and smiling at me. Twain explained that his companion, whom he called Henry, was an old friend in need of cash, a great musician and entertainer, and he asked if it would be all right if

Henry played a couple of tunes at the conclusion of the program and passed the hat so he could make his way back home. He looked me straight in the eye.

This put me in an odd position. I did not see how I could deny a request from Mark Twain, especially as he was standing in front of me. But the echoes of every faculty meeting in which I had been ridiculed with derisive epithets about "banjar" players and such, came back to me now. Twain's friend was watching me closely, and I noted a distinct ironic intelligence at play in his alert, unafraid gaze. Finally, I thought, well, what really could be the harm? Perhaps a little music at the end of the session would be a pleasant palate-cleanser.

So I answered that it would be a welcome addition, thanked Twain and his friend, and told Twain that I would see him at the dais, as soon as possible.

"Yes, of course," he said. "Let me just get Henry settled here and I'll be right up."

Five minutes later, with the panel assembled, I allowed myself a proud look at the figures assembled on that dais—my dream, realized. Here, I thought, was the true beginning of the conference. A fresh start, after the morning's mishaps. Now we would launch on the broad conversation regarding the nation's sense of purpose and how to reclaim it, with the most important writers of our time. Wasn't America the "country of beginnings"? Let us begin anew!

Cheered by this thought, once the doors were closed I stood at my place behind the dais and called the session to order. I delivered welcoming words to the near-capacity hall, making a special point of offering profuse thanks to President Withers, Provost Moreland, and Chairman Olander for their support. I stated the purpose of the session that was about to begin—a discussion of the life of the writer in America. I gave a brief acknowledgment of the six writers—Mark Twain, Herman Melville, Walt Whitman, Harriet Beecher Stowe, Lucy Comstock, and Frederick Douglass—and I announced that there would be time set aside at the end of their formal remarks for a question-and-answer session with the audience.

I introduced Mark Twain first. I had skimped on my introductions in that morning's session, assuming, incorrectly, that the attendees would be familiar with the authors' work. I would do better now. Twain's celebrity was such that he required only the broadest introduction; I mentioned his writings on the Mississippi and the West, the Gold Rush, his wonderful story about Tom Sawyer, then asked everyone to welcome him, which they did with oceanic applause. I settled in to listen with happy anticipation.

"Thank you all for that undeserved ovation," he began. "I can only assume that it was intended more for my fellow practitioners on the dais than for myself."

He took his time lighting a cigar as the audience laughed at the self-deprecating humor.

"I want to say at the outset that I did not embark on life with the intention of being a professional liar and idler—a writer, in other words. I thought perhaps I might become something noble by contrast—a category which would include just about any other activity imaginable. However, it turned out I had a facility for taking people I knew and events I had witnessed and converting them into words. I have many friends, and I have witnessed many things, and I have produced my share of words. If each of those words were a dollar I would have more money presently than J. P. Morgan. This, sadly, is not the case.

"Writers are congenital procrastinators. Every time I take the ill-advised step of commencing work on a book, fate intercedes to remind me of at least a dozen or so urgent tasks that I seem to have forgotten until that point. Naturally, these responsibilities press on one, and by answering the summons to duty I have found myself acquiring quite a facility at billiards, among other skills necessary to the well-rounded man. But in short order the knock, literal or figurative, will come upon the door and creditors will see to it that I fulfill my destiny as a professional liar once again."

I looked out across the audience, measuring the response; all seemed to be happily savoring his words. Forrest Taylor was grinning. Even Mrs. Stanford and her crew, all of whom had worn a somewhat dour aspect theretofore, appeared to be enjoying Twain's remarks. My mood brightened with every sentence Twain uttered.

"There is experience," Twain was saying, "and there is one's understanding of experience, the subjective angle upon the experience. It is this latter element that the writer is charged to deliver, because it is the one thing that he . . . or she"—and here he nodded, indicating both Mrs. Stowe and Miss Comstock—"owns outright, independent of anyone else's claim. It is the thing that makes the writer valuable, or not, and if he's lucky makes him unique. I find myself wanting to say 'necessary,' but the list of writers one might call 'necessary' could be scribbled on this napkin. In large letters, too.

"My books, unnecessary as they may be, are available at the table located conveniently outside in the lobby, to which stock has been added my newest, a reminiscence of my time on the Mississippi River. My books have been my passport to many exotic locales—to London, to the Far East, to Egypt . . . even Auburn, New York." More laughter. "I will conclude by saying that it is a great honor to share this dais with writers far greater than myself, and to whom I shall now cede the floor."

When the applause had abated I introduced Lucy Comstock. At her name, a whoop arose from her admirers, although not, I noticed, from Stanford and her group. I did my best to do Miss Comstock justice, although in all honesty I had not read her books. I concluded by saying, truthfully, that her books had brought pleasure to many readers.

Miss Comstock acknowledged the loud applause, which swelled as she stood at her seat. She was in even less of a hurry to begin than Twain had been. Chairman Olander, seated in the second row, was smiling broadly; he even proffered a discreet wave and inclined his head slightly to indicate the woman seated next to him, who was applauding ecstatically—his wife, undoubtedly.

"Thank you," Lucy Comstock said, finally, looking around the hall with a wistful smile. "Thank you ever so much. I have so enjoyed meeting so many of you this morning, and am truly humbled at hearing how much my books have meant to you. What more can a writer ask, than to know that her pages have found an enduring place in the hearts of her readers, and that her words have provided not just entertainment but even perhaps a guiding light through the thorns and thistles of life?"

The women in the audience listened raptly. The men listened politely.

"I do find myself quite atremble at being placed among these writers," Comstock went on, gesturing to the others on the panel. "My own humble works, while apparently quite popular, especially among those of my own sex—perhaps only among those of my own sex—cannot compete for lofty themes and grand adventure with the works of the men represented here. After all, the pursuit of love and marriage, the duties of a faithful wife and homemaker and helpmeet, quite pale in the strong light of ocean storms and river pilots." There was a note of sarcasm beneath the satiny surface of her words, and I noticed that Mrs. Stowe was glaring at her.

"Mr. Twain mentioned the 'necessary' writer, indicating that they were few in number—and, if I may hazard a guess, exclusively male. If I may make so bold as to say it, we are all 'necessary.' All writers, all men and all women, have their necessary story to tell, and all should be embraced."

A strong round of applause greeted these words, although a fair number of the men in the audience did not participate. Mrs. Stanford's group applauded warily; Mrs. Stanford in particular seemed to be measuring Miss Comstock's words.

"I doubt," Miss Comstock went on, "that one would argue against the 'necessity' of the woman's story were all women suddenly to absent themselves for even a day—for even one afternoon—from their designated posts as seamstress, cook, laundrywoman, floorwasher, and nursemaid. Then we might see how well the affairs of men would narrate without all the apparatus hidden behind the curtain." Now an even stronger round of applause, joined vigorously this time by Stanford herself.

"I mean no slight, of course, to the fine writers here, only to repair an imbalance in the perception of what makes a fit subject for the writer, in our time. And if I may beg your indulgence to remind you that my newest child—for my books are indeed my children—is available for purchase at the front table. *Mister Harris Proposes* is the story of Rebecca Smith's long wait and many stratagems to induce her shy suitor to propose the marriage that she so desires—which he does, although not in the manner that she—or the reader—expects. I will be so pleased to sign your copy of *Mister Harris Proposes* or, indeed, any of my volumes. Thank you."

Great applause now from throughout the hall, and polite applause from the members of the panel, excepting Mrs. Stowe, who regarded the audience with an expression somewhere between boredom and irritation.

I then introduced Herman Melville. Having persuaded him

to participate, I wanted to give him an especially laudatory tribute, and, as I was aware that his works were less known than those of the others, I spent an extra minute singing the praises of *Moby-Dick*, *The Piazza Tales*, and *Mardi*. I had not been able to make heads nor tails of *The Confidence-Man* or *Pierre*, and to my own shame I had not even looked into *Clarel*. In any case, I built him up as well as I could, and he received a respectful, if somewhat muted, ovation.

"Good afternoon!" he said, rising from his seat, grinning and bowing several times before straightening and regarding the far wall of the auditorium.

A moment passed, and then another. And then another, and several more, while he stood silently looking at the rear of the room. Just as I began to grow uneasy, he spoke again.

"I have never been much of an orator, and my lack of aptitude for promotion would be evident to anyone examining the balance sheets I receive from my publishers."

A modest wavelet of laughter greeted this remark.

Again, an interval of silence, as Melville smiled into the hall. Frowns bloomed in the front rows.

"I have found the work of the late Nathaniel Hawthorne to be of great value. I once composed an essay on his work. Archaeologists might find it in a library basement."

Now the audience was clearly, visibly puzzled. Whitman, two seats down, was writing something in a notebook, which he continued doing throughout Melville's remarks.

Suddenly, with a startling force, Melville broke into song:

> As I walked down the Broadway
> One evening in July
> I met a maid who asked my trade

And a sailor John says I.
To Tiffany's I took her
I did not mind expense
I bought her two gold earrings
And they cost me fifty cents.
And away, you Santee
My dear Annie
O, you New York girls
Can't you dance the polka. . . .

Somewhere in the hall a lone pair of hands began clapping along midway through the verse.

Melville finished as abruptly as he started, seemed on the verge of saying more, stopped himself, smiled, and said, "Thank you."

Dutiful, confused, brief applause ensued.

It was clear that he'd found something to drink during the lunch period, and I was both upset by the inappropriateness of his contribution and concerned for his state of mind. Still, the panel needed to continue; I thanked Melville and introduced Harriet Beecher Stowe, speaking mainly of *Uncle Tom's Cabin*, which had played such a part in inflaming public sentiment against slavery. I repeated President Lincoln's greeting, that she was "the little lady who had started this big war," or words to that effect. When I was finished, she rose to great applause, looking as if she were being subjected to the most odious torture.

"I don't have much to say on this subject, and I'm not sure why I am here," she began. "It never occurred to me to contrive an elaborate rationale for the work I do. I have always made up stories. When I wrote *Uncle Tom's Cabin* I was appalled at the situation the slaves were in, and I did my best with it. If I made any contribution to the end of the Peculiar Institution I am glad. I have had no say in the uses to which the characters have been put, in minstrel shows and degrading sketches, and these embarrass me. I was proud to meet President Lincoln. . . ."

She paused, and I thought it might have signaled the end of her remarks, but apparently she was simply attempting to find if she had anything to add. Which she did.

"I have continued to produce books, partly out of financial necessity, and partly because I don't seem to know how to stop writing. None of them has had the effect or, for that matter, the ambition of *Uncle Tom's Cabin.* This is fine with me. I also accept that that early book has attracted more than a few readers to my subsequent books who would likely never have sought them out, and I am grateful for that. I'd be a fool if I weren't. That's about it." Then she sat down.

The audience emitted some uncertain giggles, and then a spray of light applause.

Next it was Whitman's turn. He had continued writing in his notebook through Mrs. Stowe's remarks, which I thought quite rude. I spoke of his expansive vision of America, his loosening of the stays on the poetic line in his *Leaves of Grass,* which Emerson had called "the most extraordinary piece of wit and wisdom that America has yet contributed," and finished by reading aloud the familiar quotation from Emerson saluting him "at the beginning of a great career."

He now stood at his place, holding the notebook in which he had been scribbling and barely acknowledging the ovation he received, and without preamble began reading from the notebook.

"Auburn!" he shouted. "City of brick and quarried stone! City of clapboard and porch, city of the river and nearby lake! City of noble Seward, and noble Tubman in their turn, city of mill and foundry, waterworks, and railroad . . ."

Again there was general puzzlement, in which I shared until I realized that he was reciting a poem. Composed, apparently, in honor of the conference!

> Home to bright leaves of orange and red; home likewise to snow,
>   then budding spring, To larch and maple and willow, all in
>   their turn!
> City of high summer and white sails upon the lake, and again to
>   the turning leaves!
> Auburn of warehouse and prison, church and saloon alike,
> Courthouse and library alike, park and cemetery also alike;
> Young men in spring ripeness learning, studying—ripe, too, in
>   affection and fellowship,
> On playing field and parade ground, ample, unafraid of
>   manhood's ripeness, hearty, erect . . .

Here he tossed the notebook onto the table and continued, his face flushed and his eyes fixed on the far wall of the room.

> Thrusting . . . tumescent . . . receiving with heated breath,
> Beckoning, eye-to-eye, grateful and unafraid . . .

Twain, seated next to me, uttered the words "Oh hell" very softly. Then he stood, placed his hand gently on the poet's shoulder, and said a few words in his ear. Whitman appeared at first like one awakened from a trance; he turned his head slightly toward Twain, listening, then smiled and nodded twice.

"Thank you," Whitman said, simply, to the audience, and took his seat once again.

In the second row, Elbert Olander wore a stricken look to match that on his wife's face. Provost Moreland, seated in the first row, shot me a look of intense displeasure. What, I wondered, was making it so difficult for the writers to stay focused on the stated theme of the panel, much less the conference's broadest aims?

I had saved Frederick Douglass for last, and I prayed that he would salvage what so far had been a most disorganized and unfocused discussion. I spoke of his eloquent depiction of his hardship in his life as a slave, his profound understanding of the injustices still obtaining in the society, and his vision of the necessary path forward for the nation. He received a huge welcome, which lasted nearly twenty seconds. I noticed that General Taylor, in the second row, wore an unpleasant, mocking smile.

"I thank you for this warm reception," Douglass began. "I welcomed this invitation to speak about the role and life of a writer, because my thought, my sensibility, indeed my very freedom, has been founded on the ability to read. Through reading I found the world that lay beyond the circumscribed context into which I had been *written*, initially, by the fates and the efforts of those who wrought their advancement from the unpaid labor of myself and those whose skin color matches my own."

"*Oh, here we go. . . .*"

The remark elicited a general murmur from the hall, and audience members turned to see who had spoken. The words had come from Forrest Taylor.

With a genial smile, Taylor waved to Douglass and said, "My apologies."

"Duly accepted," Douglass said, "and doubly prized as a rare example of an apology from a representative of the late Confederacy. I was more fortunate than so many of my dark-skinned brothers and sisters in having had the opportunity to learn to read and write. This ability, which should be the birthright of every man and woman, and which was so long denied to those of my race, is held quite lightly by many who have not had to fight to claim it except in the schoolroom, whereas that birthright was grasped at the price of grievous punishment by those of my race, many of whom suffered the ultimate penalty for their efforts.

"So I will say that I cannot conceive of the place of literature in a society as being divorced from the question of citizenship in that society. Of course literature may serve as a mere entertainment, or as a necessarily temporary respite from harsh conditions. For the length of time that one is under the spell of a great writer one is absolved of the worries and concerns of the quotidian. Yet beyond this undeniable service to mankind, literature calls us—does it not?—to an awareness of our place in the world, in a society, through the summoning of the characters involved, and through our identification with them. It cannot avoid the long shadow of moral choice and responsibility."

He was undeniably brilliant as a speaker, his eloquence and his message equally compelling. Of all the participants he seemed most in tune with my conception of the conference's intent, and I was grateful to find things back on track simply through the strength of his presentation. He finished to a massive ovation.

When it was done, I announced that the authors would entertain questions from audience members regarding their books, their thoughts on literature, and the other related topics of the conference.

After some readjustments, looking around the room, hesitation, a young man stood up and said, "Would you be willing to say, where do you get your ideas?"

The panel members looked at one another. Mrs. Stowe said, "What ideas do you mean?"

"Well . . . I suppose I mean the characters . . . and what happens to them?"

"I'll take a shot at this," Twain said. "Writers get ideas from observation, experience, and imagination. Of the three, I'd say observation is the most important. If you don't have it, all the experience in the world won't do you any good. Same goes for imagination, which feeds off of your observation. Of course it goes without saying that if you don't have any experience to observe, you won't get very far, either."

"My characters," Miss Comstock offered, "are my children. I love them. You have to love your characters. I think of Eloise and Ethan in *The Mended Heart*. When I wrote the scene of their reunion after so many trials, I cried along with them. That book is available for purchase in the lobby."

I heard Mrs. Stowe shift and snort at this.

"Anyone else?" I said.

"Reading is helpful," Melville said.

A woman in the second row raised her hand and I recognized her.

"Is it very difficult to get one's book published after it is completed? Do you have any advice for those of us who hope to join your ranks?"

Lucy Comstock responded immediately. "My advice is to meet as many people as possible! Learn to smile, and don't be afraid to put yourself among those who can help you. It is hardly a secret that any man will pay more attention to a well-turned ankle than to a boring professor!" Laughter from a number of the women in the audience. "Find out where the men who make decisions take their meals!"

Clearly annoyed, Mrs. Stowe added, "It helps if you write well and work hard."

I invited the next questioner to stand.

"This is a question for Mr. Twain. You said that there weren't many necessary writers. Could you tell us which writers you would consider necessary? I mean either to your own writing, or . . . or to literature in general. Thank you." He looked as if he were about to sit down, then stood again and added, "Also if any of the other writers could tell us who has been necessary in their minds. Thank you!" And he sat down.

Twain cleared his throat and stood up. "I think that's one of the most important questions you could ask," he said. "What is necessary? I love ice cream, but I'm not sure that it is necessary, either to myself or to the continuance of civilization. There are many writers whom I enjoy reading, but whom I would not consider to be necessary, or formative. The fellows who composed the Bible have proved necessary. The Bible is the greatest compendium of fantastic lies and tall tales ever assembled—better even than the *Arabian Nights*. I don't think we could keep ourselves pasted together if it disappeared from view. Of course Shakespeare is the greatest of all writers, in English at least, and I would guess in any language. I have yet to make a traversal of writers in Sanskrit, among whom may be the one figure in world literature greater than Shakespeare."

"The Bible and Shakespeare," Melville said, "and *Paradise Lost*." He seemed to have regained his footing, and I was relieved to see it. "Another good one was Obed Macy's *History of Nantucket*. And Dana's *Two Years before the Mast*."

I saw that Lucy Comstock was directing a withering look at Melville, and I asked her to add her names.

"Well, as there have been so few—excuse me—a *complete* absence of women authors mentioned, I might cite as being necessary, to me at least, the Brontë sisters, Mary Shelley, and the novels of Jane Austen, who it seems to me stands head and shoulders above the entire pack of contemporary authors. When I was a girl I also liked the novels of Walter Scott."

I asked if Mrs. Stowe had anyone to add, and she said, "Shakespeare. And I am surprised that nobody has mentioned Mr. Douglass's *Narrative*, surely one of the 'necessary' books ever produced in America. I also liked Scott quite a bit."

"I thank Mrs. Stowe for those words," Frederick Douglass said.

"I want to add that when I was going through the difficult process not only of learning to read but of learning to shape and express my thoughts in a persuasive manner, I found a book entitled *The Columbian Orator* to be invaluable. It is a collection of dramatic sketches, speeches, *pensées*, and some poems, that would aid anyone aspiring to eloquence. I recommend it."

A man was standing in one of the rear rows, and I recognized him.

"This question is for Mr. Twain. I wonder why you decided to use the name Mark Twain on your books? Your given name was Samuel Clampitt, if I'm not mistaken."

"You are in fact mistaken," Twain said. "My given name is Clemens. Don't worry—it's an easy mistake to make. I have found, and continue to find, that it is helpful to have this other name, Twain, which precedes me into rooms of all sorts and acts as a kind of front man. People engage with him, while I have a chance to size them up."

"Doesn't that get confusing?" the man said.

"So far I've been able to keep both members of the party pretty much straight," Twain said. "Public acclaim, or fame, if you want to call it that, is never what you think it will be. It is more confusing when people are calling you by the name you were born with."

I asked if anyone else on the panel had thought to write under an assumed name.

Mrs. Stowe said, "My first publisher did suggest that my work might achieve more success if it were written, or appeared to have been written, by a man."

"Your sex does not seem to have hurt your sales, Harriet," Twain said.

"All this mystery the men talk about," Lucy Comstock said, breaking in. "Writing is not so very mysterious. Your characters speak through you, act through you, *love* through you. Sit at your desk, and let them lead you. Follow them where they go. And, I must say, unlike Mrs. Stowe, being a woman has helped me. I write for women, about things that interest women. . . ."

"*Some* women," Mrs. Stowe said, "especially those whose sole interest is in finding a husband." This elicited a surge of applause from Stanford's group, as well as some of their apparent sympathizers throughout the hall.

"Well, Mrs. Stowe," Lucy Comstock said, very sweetly, "it is clear enough that the marriage of two individuals is the entire point of society, as it ensures the continuance of the race. So, for a woman, finding a suitable husband is of the utmost importance. My latest romance, which is available for purchase outside, and which I would be pleased to inscribe, is *Her North Star*—her star being a husband who, after many a day on the sea, decides to return to land and make a home with Susannah, although it takes quite a bit of cunning on her part to induce him to do so. . . ."

"I was under the impression," Mrs. Stowe said, "that we were invited here not as farmers at a county fair who exhibit and sell their prize hogs, but to discuss matters of some import to the nation and to literature. I would also add that I know more than a few things about marriage and child-rearing. I won't presume to guess what experience Miss Comstock has had thereof. And I will also say that the late war may seem to have receded in the minds of those who have stayed insulated in the cocoon of domestic life, but it continues in thin disguise in the Southern states, where men in white hoods exact a terrible price upon any Negro who should have the temerity to claim status as fully human."

This, too, was received with strong applause from other quarters in the audience.

With even more exaggerated sweetness than before, Lucy Comstock responded, "Well, with all respect to the authoress of *Uncle Tom's Cabin*, surely there are those of us who are not exclusively preoccupied with the lives of the most wretched, and who might be forgiven for enjoying a tale now and then that bears some relation to our own experience."

"Pardon me," Mrs. Stowe said, "but are we to understand that you have been a charwoman who became miraculously wedded to a wealthy sea captain?"

"I am pleased that you are such an avid follower of my work."

"If I may wade into this," Melville said now. "I would think, Miss Comstock, that you could admit that Mrs. Stowe's themes— the enslavement of humans, the nature and costs of freedom— are themes that touch us universally, and that her book did its part to alter the course of our history."

"Well, yes, I understand, Mr. Melville," Lucy Comstock said. "Thank you for explaining that to me. And who, after all, could expect you to equally value the humble work of women who must sew and wash, and cook for men—at least as 'universal' a theme as your whaling and your war—while the men are off chasing fish, and whiskey and women along with it, never giving a thought to the women who in fact make their grand lives possible."

Applause again.

"Madam," Melville said, "may I promise you that I have spent many an hour sewing repairs in sails and swabbing decks, and even cooking for many dozens of men, all while trying my best to keep my footing amid forty-foot ocean swells. And for that matter, may I ask how the notably muscular male protagonists of your romances earned their rippling pectoral muscles if not by activities that you hold in such derision?"

At this point there was a disturbance among some of the women in the audience.

"Shame!" A woman in one of the rear rows had stood up. "Shame!"

"Shame for what?" Melville said.

"What right do you have to speak to a woman this way? Women are the equal of men, despite your condescension!"

"Madam, I—"

A man across the hall stood up and shouted at the woman, "Take your suffragist demonstration somewhere else!"

This brought a surge of remonstrance from nearly all the women in the audience. At this, Mrs. Stanford herself stood up and turned to the owner of that voice and said, "Sir, you have not seen a suffrage demonstration here. We have attended in order to understand why the most important question of our time has been ignored in this conference. So far we have come to no such understanding. At the least such a forum should raise questions, not foreclose them. Those who shout others down may be shouted down themselves. Or silenced otherwise!" And at this she raised a furled umbrella in her hand, causing laughter in the audience, as well as some shocked expressions, catcalls, cheers.

Olander was looking at me, clearly alarmed, as was Moreland, frowning, and I feared that he might be readying himself to intercede. This could not happen, so I stood and said, in a loud voice, "Ladies and gentlemen! Please! This is intended to be a discussion, not a debate, and certainly not a riot! Please! There is room for all opinions here, as long as they are delivered with respect and civility! This conference depends upon it, and so does our nation."

This, to my relief, was greeted with the strongest round of applause yet.

"Please," I continued, "let us proceed in a constructive spirit."

The shouters sat down, and most of the audience now made a demonstration of directing their attentions toward the stage. Not one minute had passed in the ensuing discussion before Mrs. Stanford and her group rose as one, made their way through their row, and left the auditorium. This was unfortunate, to say the least, but I doubted that I had heard the last from them. The discussion went on for another ten or fifteen minutes, and consisted in the main of biographical questions and workaday answers. Potentially explosive rhetoric had been traded for civility, and I wish I could say that the proceedings gained in interest thereby. The mood in the room had flattened, so to say, but at least a shut-down had been avoided.

Finally, as it was nearing five o'clock, I announced the conclusion of the panel and reminded the attendees that proceedings would resume the following afternoon, with a discussion about the future of the nation involving all the writers. As I finished my announcement audience members began standing, stretching, speaking to one another. One or two on the panel did, as well, and I was about to thank them when Mark Twain tapped me on the shoulder and said, "What about my banjo player?"

— 8 —

I HAD FORGOTTEN about the banjo player. "Of course!" I said. "I am so sorry."

"Henry's standing right over there." Twain was clearly irritated. There, indeed, was the fellow, behind the stage curtain.

The other panelists had quit the dais, and there were now a number of empty seats in the hall. Twain stepped to the front of the stage and in a loud voice announced, "Before we all go ahead and find some dinner . . ." This got the attention of the attendees, who turned to see what he was going to say. ". . . allow me to offer dessert first."

The audience members began resuming their places, or locating new ones, to hear what Twain was up to. Lucy Comstock, I noticed, had left the stage and had accepted Forrest Taylor's apparent invitation to take the empty seat next to his, several rows back. Walt Whitman and Mrs. Stowe both perched in the second aisle, near the lobby doors. And Frederick Douglass took a seat in the front row.

When the crowd had quieted, Twain gestured to the curtain and said, "Come on over here, Henry. I want you all to meet a pal of mine who I ran into on the way here. He and I hoboed our way out to California and back more than once, years ago, and his name was the stuff of legend from Carlsbad to Carson City." Twain threw in a few details about the Gold Rush, and a brief episode involving horse thieves in Colorado, as his friend made his way, slowly and stoop-shouldered, across the stage, carrying his banjo. Henry had appeared entirely alert and at ease—self-possessed, intelligent, even ironically observant—at our earlier meeting. Now I was surprised to see him walking toward the front of the stage looking like a tired field hand.

I returned to my seat at the dais, from which I could observe both the performance and the audience. Moreland threw me a stern look, to which I responded with a shrug and raised eyebrows. What was I supposed to say? Olander was frowning, although his wife appeared very happy. Forrest Taylor wore an expression of delight, like that of a boy anticipating mischief; Lucy Comstock was whispering something in his ear. In the front row, Douglass's expression was opaque, appraising—the face of a judge, I thought.

"This is Henry Sims," Twain said, "known to all by the well-deserved appellation of Banjo Henry. I want you to give him a mighty round of applause, and when he is finished I know you will all chip in whatever you can afford right here into his cap, which he has loaned to me for this purpose."

Twain pulled a silver dollar from his pocket and held it up for all to see, saying, "I will start the ball rolling," and with a flourish placed it into the cap at the front edge of the stage. "All right, Henry," he said. "Take it away." He gestured to the audience, indicating that the time for the mighty round of applause had arrived, and the only slightly emptied house complied as Twain quit the stage, leaving his protégé alone to face the crowd.

"Thank you people," Twain's friend began. "I'm mighty agitated for Mr. Train to invite me up here. I'll try to satisfy you if I can. I hope I can, because I fell off my mule two days' time ago and my shoulder got all twined up and I got the twitch in my arm . . . like a . . ." And as he said this his right hand shot to the banjo strings and played a quick scrap of melody, which ended as abruptly as it started, after only two or three seconds.

"See, there it goes. There's no telling when it's gone to act up, or how, or how long it's . . ." And he broke off again, swinging the banjo into position and snapping out another fusillade of notes, of a bit longer duration this time.

"You see what I'm telling you. And it's no use trying to stop it, and sometimes my legs start in to acting contrarywise like I had the Saint Vitus . . ." And now his legs started shaking and wobbling, as if they were independent of his upper body, and he hollered out, "You see what I'm trying to tell you . . ." and then the banjo was righted and he began to play, hollering again, "There it goes . . . ain't no stoppin' it . . . *Somebody hold my mule. . . .*" And he was off into a syncopated melody on his banjo, accompanied by an astonishing rhythmic descant from his feet. It was immediately captivating, and I could not help grinning and tapping my foot, until I remembered to comport myself. The audience, for its part, appeared almost universally delighted, and I thought that perhaps all would be well after all, until my gaze landed on Frederick Douglass, whose judgelike expression had only deepened.

When Henry finally brought the caper to an end, the crowd gave him a robust ovation. Douglass applauded, barely, but his face displayed clear displeasure.

"May I offer my profound gratitude," Henry said, quieting the crowd. "I am most indebted to you for overlooking any technical defects in my performance, attributable to my disability."

Had I heard him correctly? The crowd appeared startled by the change in his diction, none more so than myself.

"I truly am most grateful," he said, "for your generous attention."

I looked at Douglass, who was frowning, now, as if some unpleasant trick were being played. Twain, standing in the back of the hall, was drawing on his cigar with a look of satisfaction.

"Rude am I, in my speech," Henry said, "but I humbly offer now a recitation, from Shakespeare." He began declaiming in a rich, baritone voice:

> I spake of most disastrous chances,
> Of moving accidents by flood and field;
> Of hair-breadth scapes in the imminent deadly breach;
> Of being taken by the insolent foe;
> And sold to slavery, and my redemption thence,
> And with it all my travel's history. . . .

Henry had changed aspect yet again, and as he spoke the very atmosphere in the room changed; the audience sat as if in a trance. He finished with the lines,

> And often did I beguile her of her tears,
> When I did speak of some distressed stroke
> That my youth suffered; my story being done,
> She gave me for my pains a world of sighs.

And here he broke off and hung his head down for a long moment during which the entire hall seemed to stop breathing. Then he raised his head, his countenance changed, and he smiled and bowed a proper theatrical bow, as the crowd thundered its appreciation.

I noticed Douglass wiping his eyes with a kerchief.

"When I have finished my next selection," Henry went on, "I will beg your indulgence in abetting my return journey to Omega Farm by depositing any modest amount you might be able to spare in that cap there. It's got a few holes in it, but I'll be careful picking it up. The text of this particular recitative is taken from an unpublished manuscript by Rabelais. Like many of you, I am certain, I love me some chicken, and I hope, and trust, that this encomium to the fair fowl will meet with your full approval."

Henry once again pulled his instrument into position before

the bewildered audience and began an almost stately melody of an introductory character, grinning and looking from side to side at the entranced spectators. Then he began singing:

> I had a dream last night
> It almost scared me white
> I dreamt that hens and roosters grew on trees. . . .

It was a fantasia of abundance, in which chickens nested in trees and hopped into frying pans of their own volition, where they were browned and basted and consumed with ecstatic pleasure. The tune was so fetching, and his banjo playing so apt and rhythmic, that the audience was clapping along to the song within a minute. And when he reprised the refrain a second time, the audience sang along with great gusto:

> It was under the chicken tree,
> Under the big fricassee,
> Eggs was droppin'
> From every blossom;
> I lost all my taste for the meat they call possum.

I saw Taylor and Lucy Comstock swaying back and forth in their seats, singing along as well.

Douglass sat in granitic silence.

The song was finished and bedlam ensued as Twain's friend bowed meekly, reverting to his original stage posture. By the time Twain had run to the front, plucked the cap off the edge of the stage, and was collecting donations, Douglass had left his seat and was walking quickly toward the exit.

I jumped up from my chair and ran after him, elbowing through the crowd as it pressed toward the stage, and I caught up with him as he was about to leave the auditorium.

"Mr. Douglass," I said, "please wait. Are you all right? You seemed upset by the presentation. . . ."

He turned and regarded me with eyes that might have melted iron. "Upset?" he said. "The word implies an equilibrium disturbed. No, not by a variation on such a familiar theme. I had the impression that I had been invited here to participate in a serious discussion of our national situation. And instead I find this relic of the subjugation and debasement of my race, presented as entertainment. I could withstand the vulgar 'question-and-answer,' but this is an insult, and I will be leaving."

"Wait . . . please," I said, in a panic. "I had no idea . . . I took him for an indigent whom Mr. Twain was trying to help. I thought he would perform outside and attendees would spare him some coins and that would be an end of it. This was not meant to be part of the program. Please . . . your presence is central, and tomorrow's discussion will be focused exclusively on the issues of the nation's future. It cannot happen without your voice. . . ."

I saw him soften just a bit, most likely from pity. In his eyes, I now realize, I had become one more well-meaning yet oblivious white man. I reflect on the deep irony that it was the pride of my race to believe that his race, supposedly childlike and credulous, needed guidance and care, when in fact the members of his race regarded the white race, with its delusions and blindness, with a mirroring belief, only with more justification.

At any rate, he quieted me, unsmiling but no longer at the boiling point. He said that he was going to have dinner with Mrs. Tubman and that he would likely stay if I would afford him the time to collect himself. Then he walked away.

I was relieved, but I had been shaken by the entire episode. I walked back inside, where the crowd had thinned out somewhat, with quite a few people gathered close to the stage, listening to

Twain expound on something. As I was surveying the room a hand landed on my shoulder, and its owner's voice said, "Congratulations on an excellent finale to the day." It was Forrest Taylor. "A fine variation on Hamlet's play. I hadn't taken you for an ironist."

I stammered, "I don't know what you mean."

He seemed about to respond when Miss Comstock called to him; he looked at her, signaled, then said to me, "Further laurels to be strewn anon," and stepped away.

−9−

MARK TWAIN GAVE HENRY a ride back to the fairgrounds, where they shared a drink from a bottle that Charlie had stashed under some rigging, then he headed off up the midway to spend some time in the land of eternal youth. He had loved the circus and the carnival since he was a boy. The feeling of possibility, to be had for a penny to the tune of the calliope, the carnival's heroic muse. The same moments and the same types repeated themselves always and everywhere, a *commedia dell'arte* amid the lamplit amusements. There was the man with the mighty arm in the jacket and loosened cravat, aiming and missing, aiming and missing; there was the Ferris wheel of time that lifted fortunes and dropped them through the twinkling screams of fear and delight. There the gymnast sprang from the trampoline, with a nip and a tuck, landing and spreading his arms with a triumphal smile, and there was the man who walked through fire, who rode two horses at once, there the elephant by the canvas tent wall, raising and lowering its long grey truth. And Lincoln in blackface recites the Gettysburg Address on the boards by the gaslights as the sun drains away and the indigo sky reclaims itself and it is all the kingdom of after, or before, and the carousel is the world and there is a woman with muscles and a beard, and there is Zazel and her sequins. . . .

Only two months before, he had resumed work on the raft novel that he had set aside for several years. An endless midway—that was the river, and all the river towns. If he could have done so, he would have let that river continue forever, in a never-ending idyll. But where was the ending; where was the bill that must always be presented? Seeing Frederick Douglass and Henry in the same setting had brought the question back to him, unexpectedly. What would the boy Huck do, finally, about his friend? Like the boy, the author was deferring that judgment as long as possible.

———

As we walked up and down in the dark blue so mystic,
As we walked in silence the transparent shadowy night . . .

Whitman had composed the lines years earlier, on the Brooklyn ferry, gazing at Venus hanging low in the western night sky; he recited them now under the tender stars along the midway to the young man walking next to him.

He had offered Lemuel Fowler a half dollar to accompany him to the fairgrounds, and the young man, his responsibilities ended for the day, had not known how to demur. But the good grey poet fretted, now, that he was not keeping the boy amused. So as they strolled past the booths and the games and the peep shows he spoke of his memories, the lamps along the Battery, the fishermen's buoy-lights bobbing in the current, the trains in the distant yards shifting in their uneasy repose, and in the vault of the blue-black evening the stars so clear, all the world of appearance, beckoning the mind and heart toward the great mystery underneath. . . . The midway teased him, brought to mind the Broadway of his youth; the thought brightened his mood, a gay moment's conceit, and he asked the young man if he enjoyed the theater.

"I have never been."

"Never?" Whitman said. "Oh, but you must go."

So he told the young man, proudly, and with starlit nostalgia, of Hackett at the old Park, of Tom Hamblin and Charles Kean, and Henry Placide in *Cinderella*. He had seen Fanny Kemble in *Fazio, or, The Italian Wife*, and the great Booth, especially as Pescara in *The Apostate*; the Bowery Theater, Edwin Forrest, all the forgotten plays—*The Iron Chest, Andromaque*, and the operas, the Italians he favored, Verdi, hearing the great Alboni . . . the names flying by like scraps of paper in the wind, tangled like unsorted receipts on an old man's floor . . . and he knew the young man was likely bored, or wishing to be elsewhere, and he thought of his darling Harry, the ring he had given, the sad goodbyes . . . and a pang of absence and regret overwhelmed him, the same wound, always, and without thinking, his hand, at his side, reached out to the young man walking beside him, and the young man's hand did not withdraw. It was all he needed under the lamplight of the heavens. . . .

The afternoon's panel had left Frederick Douglass unsettled, the more so after the episode of the banjo player and the ensuing exchange with the organizer. He felt the need to walk off his mood before his visit with Twain, and now he strolled slowly down the midway alongside Harriet Tubman, his friend and host for the week-end, past the games and the sideshows.

"I spoke too sharply to the young man in charge," he was saying. "I feel badly. I was disappointed, I suppose. I thought he might have considered the occasion more fully."

"How many white people do you know?" his friend said.

"I don't think Twain meant any harm or slight. He wanted to help his friend, and he did not think the moment through."

Music wafted toward them as they walked, an illuminated mist; the tune was "Carnival in Venice," played by a strolling hurdy-gurdy man accompanied by a monkey on a string. The monkey wore a maroon fez, and it approached them, chittering and holding out a cup, as they passed.

"I bought a violin in London," Douglass said.

"You can play the violin?"

"I play it," Douglass responded. After a few more moments, Douglass added, "Please come with me to Twain's this evening." He added, "I think you might steady me. I have looked forward to this visit. For relief, do you understand?"

"Relief?"

They heard rapid footfalls behind them; someone approaching quickly, and the words "Mr. Douglass. . . ."

They both turned, and Douglass was taken aback to see the banjo player from that afternoon's performance, out of breath and bent over, now, from the exertion, regaining his breath, hands on his knees, looking briefly at the hay-strewn ground. Even in the dim evening by the small lights in the booths, Douglass could see the man's green eyes, light complexion, grey-flecked hair, yet with a boyish aspect: the foreclosed youth, always that recognition.

"Please excuse me," Henry said. "I wanted to greet you at the program, but it was impossible. . . . I just wanted to say I met you. Thank you. . . . Thank you for everything."

Just after nightfall, thinking of gayer times, Herman Melville donned a light jacket and exited his room at Harmony House. The banjo player's performance at Midlake had lifted the lid on a sleeping spirit, and he had decided to attend the carnival. As he shut the door behind him he had a second thought; the night was cool, and he feared the chill.

He entered his room again, removed the light jacket and put

on his other, heavier, jacket, added a scarf which Elizabeth had insisted that he pack, and quit the room once more, descended the stairs and crossed the foyer, walked past the sitting room, where a fire had been started, and stepped outside.

On the building's front steps, looking across the grounds, he felt the slight chill at the roots of his scalp. The going-out, but then the coming-back. Anticipation, but then the reckoning. How had you spent your time, who was watching, and was it better if there were a Being, or if there were no one, and so the lights and the games . . . can you accept . . . can you breathe it in, and then breathe it out . . . a small Indian doll . . . there was a lightning storm in his mind . . . he could not.

He turned and entered the house again, closed the front door, and walked again past the sitting room and back to the stairway, where he paused. He imagined himself alone in his room, by the wavering candle. And what was the point, then, in having come if he might as well have been home.

He turned, again, feeling the point of the sword at his back, and walked out the front door, heard it close behind him, walked quickly across the grounds to the Institute gate, through which he had rode in the carriage only the day before, exited and stood on the sidewalk under the stars, looking left and right. Drawing a deep breath, he turned to the right and began to proceed downtown, where he might find a hack and go to the carnival. Alone, a sentimental trip to a past from which he had been exiled as surely as Adam from the Garden. What memories might be summoned? A trip with his son? Remembered the question Malcolm had asked, about the moon.

He halted on the sidewalk. Phases the same as faces. So alone. No.

He walked quickly back through the Institute gates and fairly ran through the silent campus, entered the house once again, careful to slow his pace in case anyone were present, walked through the foyer breathing heavily and ascended the steps.

Once in his room, with the door closed and locked, he removed the jacket and laid it across the bed, pulled out the chair at the little desk and sat down with his head in his hands. The lady writer taking aim at him; where was the point of any of it. Countess Faustina in the image of Lula. . . . A disgrace to the House of von Hahn-Hahn . . . Disputation to be left to the Rabbinate. Or the Inquisitors. The voices insisting, the futility of it all. To take one side and suffer the centrifugal comeuppance, thrown off the carousel.

He had brought two lengths of thin hemp line for pass time, and he picked them up. May it not be said that he forgot in the cabin what he learned in the forecastle. Half hitch, clove hitch . . . On the *Acushnet* they called the clove the "button." Out of sight of land. Meditation worthy of the fakir. Never cared for scrimshaw; the empty page had been his virgin ivory. His arena for the knots he devised. The knot achieved, the little ships in the bottles, sent out, properly corked. His vintage spoiling in the attic. Now only jams and jellies. He had lost the Lever book with the beautiful drawings of the knots. *Sheet Anchor.* Somewhere, fathoms down.

Slip knot. The rope stretching downward, as the spirit climbs. His son, beautiful, and blameless. What if the boy could not utter whatever had beset him, struck back at the mute cause and so sealed his fate. . . . Final acceptance, the knee taken. No man lonelier, but what if he met his God in acceptance. Was there ever a man who on the gallows blessed the hanging judge? But hadn't He asked forgiveness for His persecutors? Was that peace, at last? Blameless boy. Peace at last.

He was vibrating. A rhythm was insisting upon itself. From his portfolio he retrieved a sheet of paper, then picked up a pen and wrote the words "Fathoms down."

He stared at the words. Outside the window, the moon.

"*Fathoms down, fathoms down.*"

He stared at the words. Who are you?

Bound there, at the wrists.

"*Ease the darbies.*"

Or "*Ease these darbies at the wrist.*"

He stared at the words. They glowed and pulsed. The words stared back at him.

The twilight promised secrets. She strolled, unsure whether she witnessed life or life's camouflage, a temporary exile. Night housed the two eternities that crowded in upon the common dream. She had seen the woman disappear in the box, the lurid façades.

Earlier, following the afternoon's program, she had retreated to the rooming house, away from the contending energies at the auditorium. A latch had turned in her at the sight of the young man in charge of the proceedings, begging for civility. As well, she thought, brandish a sword against the tides. He had taken up a residency in her affections, and she was restless. Beardless, he was, and a persistent lock of hair.

Outside her room the carnival's wagons and carts bally-hooed along the streets, proclaiming gaiety and offering transport, echo of the circus that had once passed her window in Amherst. Would these carts carry that memory away now with finality? Would the young man be in attendance? The impulse was overwhelming; she wrapped herself quickly, walked outside, and hailed one. Love, perhaps, had made her reckless. Wasn't that its purpose? Riding in the cart was itself a rare morsel; did the angels feel so motionless as they flew through the ether? Would they recognize themselves?

I was potted, in a word. A reporter potted is a reporter on a horse.

This last, cryptic observation I had entered into my notebook while sitting, restless and potted, at one of the Echo Tavern's long tables, wondering how I might force a newsworthy item for the *World* out of the day's non-events. The only liveliness had been provided by Twain's colored friend. I thought the ladies of Seneca Falls might heat things to a boil, but young Matthews had interceded. For a moment I thought Whitman might disrobe at the dais while reciting his hilarious "poem," but that newsworthy display never quite left the gate.

Over my third pint I considered how pleasant it must be to install oneself at a dais and dispense pomposities for the credulous public and the fawning acolytes. Unfortunately I found it necessary to earn a living. At every turn of the afternoon discussion I imagined a rejoinder superior to anything the panel's eminences proffered. I was restless and potted, and at length—the length of four pints and two small glasses of whiskey—I resolved to attend the carnival. It was billed as a circus, but a carnival without a ring was not a circus. It was a carnival. You may have riders, you may have an elephant, but it is not a circus without a ring. Circus equals circle, God damn them all to hell. I set my final, empty, pint glass down loudly on the table, exculpated myself from the bench—the word is "extricated" and to hell with you, too—and proceeded to the fairgrounds.

I walked in the sights as I drank along the midway, rather I drank in the sights, et c, under the potted violets of evening. I can write like that if I wanted. I could pitch balls at stuffed toys, thanks, if I wanted. I was a walking itch. I imagined Broadway, with its electric stars shining upon me. There the streets were numbered, implying progress; here the booths attracted the unwary flies, but with no sequence; they could have been arranged in any order. This idea sustained me and proved my brilliance. I was summoned to Broadway and progress. I was never complete without incompletion. Wanting something is the beginning of time. I was not disabled; I was merely illuminated.

And by my lights, down the way, to my astonishment, I saw proof of my electability. I quickened my pace, and approaching saw that it was indeed Mark Twain. As if by the inscrutable decree! Here, now, was my chance to correct my *faux pas* of the morning and offer him the greetings from his *amour*, the coquettish Tilley, which I had forgotten to convey earlier, my proof of citizenship in the brotherhood, a confidential messenger, privy to the passwords. . . . I approached him from behind and put my hand, gently I thought, on his forearm.

He pivoted quickly, jerking his arm away, and I cringed, expecting a blow. But he had planted himself and faced me, and I filled the moment by reintroducing myself and reminding him of our meeting that morning.

"Right," he said. "Good to see you." He nodded and made as if to continue on without me.

"Wait," I said. "I have a message from you. *For* you, I mean." He stopped, turned to me once again, and waited for me to deliver the message.

"I'm writing a notice for the New York *World*, and my editor wanted you to know that 'Tilley sends her greetings.'" I gave him a hearty, complicitous smile. I might even have winked.

He showed no sign of comprehension.

"Who?" he said.

"Tilley?" I said. "The editor wired to tell you that Tilley sends regards . . . ?" I had demoted the writer of the wire from "my" editor to "the" editor.

"Tilley?" he said. "Oh . . ." And here his face broke into a broad smile. "At the *World*?" He laughed, a great laugh that I knew must be at my expense. "That's Frank Tilley," he said. "My old St. Louis pal. I heard he was at that new rag. . . . Tilley sends greetings! That is rich!" He was laughing as if he had heard the funniest joke imaginable, and I was the joke. He regained himself and, still smiling happily, said, "Tell Tilley I send kisses, and a bouquet will follow. Thanks for the greetings, pal." He clapped me on the shoulder, as he had that morning. "I'm looking for somebody. Good to see you." And again he turned away from me and proceeded in the general direction of the carousel as I stood there with Broadway fading in the insuperable distance.

To my immediate right was a stall with stuffed dolls arrayed on shelves, and the slouched boy waiting for the next hero. Without portfolio I approached, placed my penny on the ledge, and he obliged me by placing three of the large balls in a tray on said ledge. I thanked him and picked up two of the balls in my right hand, and the other in my left.

"Watch this," I said, and with both hands threw them all at once, and the balls one and all ricocheted off the wooden shelves and caromed onto the floor.

"Tell them about me," I said, and I walked off into the aboriginal gloom.

Twain made his way slowly toward the fairgrounds exit, past the wooden livestock stalls, the gypsies, a man with a ruby in his ear.

Douglass would be coming for the promised drinks and cigars, and he needed to get back to Harmony House. Hearing Tilley's name had set off a very agreeable detonation of nostalgia.

Some paces behind him a woman walked, watching him. Saw him from a distance, walking, alone, and she was certain. He was ambling, seemingly lost in thought, and following her impulse she caught up and called to him from behind and saw him stop and deflate, slightly. Turning half-way around, he said, "You found me out."

"I only wanted to say I met you," she said. "I write poems."

He gave her a long gaze, and in the half light of the gas lamps she could not tell if it was a sad look or a pleased one. He patted her shoulder and walked away.

–10–

ALTHOUGH I WAS NEARLY exhausted after the day's exertions, the undercurrents of tension at the session, the bizarre episode with Twain's banjo player, and then a dinner during which I nearly fell asleep in my chair, I decided that I ought to stop into Harmony House to make sure that all was well. It was surprisingly chill for a June night, and I arrived to find a fire going in the small parlor and, to my great surprise and delight, Mark Twain sitting with Frederick Douglass and a short, dark-skinned woman whom I recognized after a moment to be Harriet Tubman. I was so pleased, and taken aback, to find Douglass there, and in converse with Twain, no less, as I was quite afraid that the episode with the banjo player had broken Douglass's desire to participate, despite his reassuring words. But here they were, with glasses in hand and cigars alit.

Twain and Douglass greeted me warmly; Mrs. Tubman, across the room, nodded at me and held up a brown hand. She didn't smile, nor did she seem displeased; I had the impression of a being who wasted as little energy as possible upon any unnecessary words or actions. The wave, then, was equal to an ovation, and I was flattered.

"Sit down, young man," Twain said, "and pour yourself some of Taylor's brandy. We are just telling some stories, trying to see who can catch whom out in the biggest lie."

"Do not be surprised," Douglass said, "if you see Twain emerge with the laurel crown."

"You're too steeped in the truth, Fred," Twain said. "I got you beat by a mile when it comes to making things up."

"We shall see," Douglass said, and the two men clicked glasses.

"Mrs. Tubman," I said, reaching for the brandy decanter, "may I pour you some brandy?"

"No thank you," she said.

I poured a modest amount for myself as Twain began speaking.

"This is, in point of fact, a true story. Or I should say factual; every man may discover his own truth in it. When the Alberts line was in its infancy I worked for a season on its run between St. Louis and New Orleans. Its crown jewel was the steamboat *Rainbow*, which was fitted out to the utmost at least partly in an effort to entice wealthy patrons—not just from our country but from Europe.

"In this they were quite successful, and in my tender years I received a liberal education in the ways of the cosmopolitan world. We had many Englishmen, Frenchmen, Germans, Austrians, and Italians, and a sprinkling of Croatians and Portuguese. Among them all, the Germans enjoyed a reputation for being both the most exacting in their expectations of service and the most reserved in their bestowals of emoluments upon those charged with serving them. In consequence, we tended to consider them a nuisance, constantly petitioning us for the smallest adjustments in their comfort. It was a commonplace among us that if a German wished his shaving mug moved three quarters of an inch to one side on his dresser, he would call to us rather than move it himself.

"At this time, a significant portion of the *Rainbow*'s route took us through the lower reaches of the Mississippi River, which are justly acclaimed for the variety of their native flora and fauna. We would often be buttonholed on our way from one errand of service to answer questions regarding the foliage and the wildlife. 'What is that strange tree?' 'It is a cypress, Madam.' 'What is that unusual bird?' 'That is a pelican.' And so forth. Never did they complain of the heat, nor the mosquitoes, or some of the country odors that we would occasionally pass through. The Germans were exacting, but they were stoic.

"One of the women in this particular party of Germans was traveling alone. She was a classic example of the type, attractive and vital even in middle age, and she had come to check America off of her list of ways to dispose of the money left her by her late husband. She complained about nothing, but she would enlist our services if she found a wrinkle in her coverlet. One evening as I was rushing to deliver a third bottle of champagne to a group of rowdy Frenchmen she hailed and detained me. I politely asked what I could do for her. She responded, very stoically and quietly, 'Zere is a lissard in my lavatory. I should like someone to remove it.'

"I had been interrupted so many times that evening by demands for my services that I was a bit less chivalrous than I might have been otherwise, and I responded, 'Madam, those *lissards* are friendly little creatures that mean no harm. In fact they do us a service by eating annoying insects. They may easily be picked up and placed outside on the balcony of your stateroom with no harm either to you or the lissard.'

"'Yes,' she said, 'I do not think so easy. You will please remove it.'

"I let her know that I was in the middle of several pressing errands, but that I would check with her later and if the lissard was still threatening her I would pick it up in a napkin and make a pet of it myself. Then I delivered the champagne to the French.

"I went to bed that evening quite exhausted, having forgotten completely about the German lady's request, and certain, when I remembered it in the morning, that the lizard had by then decamped of its own volition, given how unwelcoming had been its reception. That day's duties commenced early and proceeded without a letup. Twice I was enjoined, with another steward, to move a grand piano from one end of a ballroom to the other; we also raised two voluminous chandeliers to make headroom for a group of tumblers, and we teamed up to deliver several cases of champagne to the French. My partner and myself had finally taken refuge with the intention of gaining for ourselves a few blessed moments of reprieve, when I heard the familiar voice and turned to see her again, as she said, 'If you haf time I would like ze lissard removed from my lavatory. This is not right that it takes so long; it is quite an inconfenience. . . .'

"My partner said to me, 'What does she want?'

"'She's got a lizard in her bathroom,' I said.

"'Why doesn't she throw it outside herself if it's bothering her?'

"'Madam,' I said, 'this is the first rest we have had all day. I promise you that when we have had a chance to catch our breath we will come and remove your lizard.'

"'It has taken so long a time,' she said.

"'Please go back to your room, and we will be there in but a few moments.'

"She nodded, unhappily, and walked away.

"'What's the big deal,' my partner said. 'Why don't you just go get the damn lizard and toss it yourself?'

"'First of all, I'm tired,' I said, handing him one of the two oranges I had swiped from the kitchen. 'Second of all, I don't see why she can't do it herself. Everybody talks about how stoic the Germans are, how they endure everything without complaint, unruffled by anything, yet they expect you to hand them a kerchief within ten seconds of every sneeze.'

"We finished our oranges, and my partner generously offered to accompany me to the lady's cabin, where we would collaborate on the eviction of the lizard. A scant two minutes later we arrived on the luxury deck, at the door of what I knew to be one of the finest cabins on the boat. We knocked, and the door opened instantly; she must have been standing right by it. She led us in without speaking, holding herself as if her arms were cold. My partner preceded me into the lavatory, and as I was about to tell the woman that we would be through in a moment and she could see how harmless the lissard was, I heard my partner loudly emit a familiar expletive in an unmistakable tone of shock and alarm. I entered the bathroom and saw, wedged under the clawfoot bathtub, the largest alligator I have ever seen. I repeated my partner's expletive, and may have added one or two of my own. We both backed out of the lavatory, and our hostess guilelessly asked us, 'It is a big lissard?'

"'Yes, ma'am, it is. Very big. We will need to call for some assistance.'

"As it turned out the alligator was unconscious, most likely from knocking its head on the tub's bottom. Why it had not been reported by one of the chambermaids is a worthwhile question, although perhaps the chambermaid who discovered it jumped overboard in a panic.

"The lady was offered many apologies, and I left the Alberts line shortly thereafter for less hazardous employment as a sword-swallower."

"What happened with the alligator?" Douglass asked.

"Three fellows had to go in and somehow remove it from its wedged-in position without getting themselves chewed to pieces, and I believe that the creature was remanded to its native environment without much further ado."

"That is quite an interesting story," Douglass said. "It begs comparison as an ethnographic study with the temperamental qualities of the British, in an episode that I witnessed with my own eyes."

Twain was lighting a new cigar, with evident pleasure. I did not smoke, but I poured myself some more brandy from the decanter on the table and settled in to listen.

"During a stay in the West Indies," Douglass began, "in one of my postbellum respites from lecturing, I found myself a guest at a fine estate outside Port-au-Prince. As on your *Rainbow*, the company at this estate was the cream of society, and I was enlisted as a kind of ambulatory cabinet of curiosities."

Twain laughed at this.

"There was a good bit of wildlife, mostly completely harmless, at this estate. Little birds, insects, oddments of this or that phylum of mammalia, among which was a monkey, who bothered no one at all except this one particular Englishwoman. Apparently she excited quite a reaction in him, and he responded by making a nuisance of himself, stealing food from off her table at the outdoor dining area, and sometimes directly off her plate when she was eating. She tried shushing the monkey away, but he was one persistent monkey."

"Wouldn't take no," Twain said.

"Wouldn't take no," Douglass repeated. "One of the stewards, a fine-looking Haitian Negro, passing by the table, noticed this interaction and, gently clapping his hands, said softly, but firmly, 'Bad monkey!' and the monkey backed off to the perimeter of the dining area.

"The next day, at breakfast, the woman was at her place, and the monkey resumed his raids upon her plate. Once again, she tried shooing the monkey away, but he would only back up a foot or so and wait for her to go back to eating and he would approach again for another raid. And once again the steward, noticing the scene, gently clapped his hands and said, in a voice soft yet firm, 'Bad monkey!' and the monkey withdrew.

"After her meal she sought this steward out and asked him if there were anything to be done about this monkey. It was wearing on her nervous state, and she was quite agitated, and she averred that she had been quite wound up on account of this problem. The steward reassured her—he had to do it several times—that the monkey meant no harm and presented no threat to her, but if he was being a nuisance all she needed to do was clap her hands as she had seen him do, and say, 'Bad monkey!' and the monkey would withdraw.

"Well, this woman repeated the advice over and promised herself that she would do it at her very next meal. But she had invested this monkey with so much malevolent intent, he had gotten to her so, that she was quite nervous about executing the plan. The steward gently told her not to worry, and that it was the only way to handle the monkey. She rehearsed it in her mind—she had, after all, seen the results—and the next morning, after losing quite a bit of sleep from worry, there was the monkey again, on her very table, staring her right in the eye, as if he had stepped out of a dream to torment her. Now with a mixture of fear and angry resolution she mustered all her courage and, slapping her hands together loudly three times, shouted '*BAD MONKEY!*' Whereupon the monkey leaned forward directly in her face and with a hideous leer screamed '*EEEEEEEEEEH!*' The woman shot to her feet, knocking the table over, and ran to the steward for help.

"'I did just as you said,' she said. 'And he screamed at me!'

"The steward gave her a reproachful look and said, 'Madam, one should never overstate the obvious when dealing with intelligent animals.'"

Laughter all around, and I thought I might have seen just a faint spark of competitive jealousy in Twain's eyes. Douglass was looking at Harriet Tubman, and said, "Harriet?"

"I'm pleased to sit and listen," she said.

I saw something pass between them, and Douglass said, "I think it is fine."

I looked around the parlor; it was warm, the lamps were low but not too low, and the brandy warmed the spirits but did not overheat them, and as there were in the room only the four of us, I took him to be saying that she should feel free to speak as she wished.

"Give us a story," Douglass said. "Isn't it written that one should not hide one's light under a bushel?"

"Mrs. Tubman," Mark Twain said, "if I make a solemn vow not to repeat the story or reveal its provenance, would that encourage you?"

"See what he said, Harriet?" Douglass said. "First he said he wouldn't repeat it, but then if that's true why is he saying he wouldn't reveal its provenance? Watch out for these double-dealing riverboat men."

All three laughed at this, and, with her guard now sufficiently lowered, or her bushel sufficiently raised, Harriet Tubman moved her chair closer to the center of the circle.

"All right," she said. "One day this preacher was riding his horse and he passed by a farm. Inside the fence he saw there was a pig with a wooden leg. The farmer was standing out there in the pen, so the preacher pulled up by the fence and said, 'Excuse me, brother, but why does that pig have a wooden leg?'"

As she spoke these words, I heard the front door of Harmony House open, then shut, and into the parlor walked Forrest Taylor, who surveyed the room and greeted us with the odd ironic aspect that I had come to see as his trademark.

"Hello, Taylor," Twain said. "Your brandy is right there."

"I thank you," Taylor said. "Unseasonable chill outside. I'd hoped to find some relief from it in here." He said this looking ironically at Douglass and Harriet Tubman, neither of whom greeted him. "Brandy it is, then."

"I hope you'll forgive us if we take our leave," Douglass said, rising from his chair. "Mrs. Tubman and I should make our way back to her house for the evening."

"Won't you stay?" I said. "Mr. Douglass, you have a room set aside for you, and I believe there is at least one extra room in which Mrs. Tubman might be comfortable for the night." Behind me I thought I heard Taylor draw a sharp breath.

"Thank you," Douglass said. "Very kind of you, on both our accounts. But we will be going. We will see you at tomorrow's program." He shook my hand, nodded at Taylor as he walked past him, and gave Twain a handshake and a clap on the shoulder. Harriet Tubman walked past Taylor without a word, then nodded at Twain, who walked her to the door, saying something in her ear that I could not hear.

"Well," Taylor said, brightly, when we were alone in the room. "That was quite a civilized little meeting, wasn't it?" He removed his jacket and hung it upon a rack. "Theoctitus received a similarly revealing greeting in the Roman marketplace from Glaucus, the slave he had freed. Odd how they petition for an equal place in a society to which they have no intention of contributing as equals. More brandy for you?" He held out the decanter, tilted toward my glass.

Twain walked back into the room. "Raining now, too. Pretty sorry little barouche she had; I offered to send for my own man but they declined. How are you, General?"

"Does she live here in town?" Taylor asked.

"I believe just south of town. Seward secured the house and land for her. She sells pies and whatnot to support her compound."

"Ah," Taylor said. "The Moses of her people. I am well, I suppose. Did I tell you," he said to me, "that Mr. Harris sends his regrets and is looking forward to my dispatches from the conference?"

"Thanks," I said. "I wish he could have been here." After a moment, I added, "In addition to you, I mean."

"Yes, of course," Taylor said. Then, resuming his address to Twain, he said, "My wife has been ill. After this week-end I will need to go back to Richmond and see after her. How is the Connecticut Confederate's life proceeding?"

"Just fine, Forrest. You know, I wish you could have been here to hear the story Douglass just told. I was set back on my heels. He all but made me sign an affidavit swearing never to repeat it."

"By which agreement I am certain you will abide for at least the duration of this conference. At any event I doubt that anyone in this room would have heard the anecdote had I been present. Wonderful manners they have."

Twain pulled a cigar out of his waistcoat, glanced at me sideways, and said, "Are you not smoking?" He removed the band and clipped the end with an instrument he had in his pocket.

"No," I said, "I can't count it among my vices." This last phrase was a direct imitation of Twain's speaking style, and I realized that the brandy was having its effect on me.

The two men exchanged an amused look as Twain lit his cigar. Again we heard the front door open, and a man's voice saying, quietly, "We will be upstairs," and as they passed the door of the parlor I saw that it was Walt Whitman, accompanied, to my great surprise, by Lemuel Fowler. Upon noticing me in the room, Fowler froze, with a look of shock on his face. Whitman took in the situation at a glance, turned to Fowler, and said, "Thank you so much for showing me the way, Mr. Fowler. I would certainly have lost it on my own. Good night to you. Unless, of course, you would care to join us in the parlor . . ."

"No," Fowler said, with his voice barely under control. "Hello, Professor Matthews. I was walking Mr. Whitman home. Good night to you!"

"I will see you out," Whitman said to Fowler.

"No!" Fowler said. "It is quite all right! I will . . . I will see you tomorrow. Goodbye!" And he caught his jacket on the door-knob and Whitman freed it for him as he took a very hurried leave.

Twain and Taylor were clearly amused by the situation and the exchange, and Whitman seemed not perturbed in the slightest. He walked into the room, said "Hello" all around, and seated himself next to me on the couch. Directing his attention to me, he said, "Are you satisfied with the conference, so far?"

His way was so peculiar, so completely his own; I noted again the sense of immediate intimacy he generated, the dispensing with formalities, no preamble, the direct address. . . .

"Yes," I said. "It feels like a dream. To have imagined it and then to see it come into being, and to meet you all, and Mr. Melville . . ."

"How do you feel the public aspect has gone, so far," Forrest Taylor asked me. He always seemed to be steering for a point, even when asking a question, and I found myself bristling slightly.

"Beyond my hopes," I said. Then, "How do *you* think it has gone, so far?"

I heard Twain emit a short bark of a laugh, and then he said, "Swordsmanship."

"And against a horseman," Taylor said to him.

"Were you in the cavalry, indeed?" Whitman said.

"I directed cavalry, sir," Taylor said. "Young man, I greatly enjoyed some sequences in the day's progress, and found myself inclined to catch up on my sleep during others. I must say that Twain's colored friend provided the greatest stimulus, with his banjar, and I believe the audience's response served as my imprimatur in the matter. He is an unusual specimen. Where did you find him?"

"He is not quite who he appears to be at first, is he?" Whitman said. Then, to me, he said, "May I?" gesturing to the brandy decanter, which was just beyond his reach on the table. I handed it to him along with a fresh glass from the tray.

"Nobody is," Twain said, holding out his hand for the decanter as Whitman finished pouring. "He's from all over, which is where I first met him."

Taylor laughed at this.

"I would be most curious to speak with him directly," Whitman said. "The fact that he mixed his diction in that way was uncanny."

"Common thing on the river, Walt," Twain said. "Characters who can declaim Shakespeare at one moment and curse like a stableboy at the next. You know that."

"Yes, of course," Whitman said. "And not just upon the river. But I mean . . . well . . . Is he still about?"

"Not sure," Twain said. "I think he raked in enough money to commence a world tour."

"The money will be gone in a few days," Taylor said, "if he conforms to type."

"That is a cruel remark," Whitman said. "Nothing about him conformed to type, Forrest."

"Well," Taylor said, "perhaps I am conforming to type, then."

A pause in the conversation. Taylor seemed to be regrouping his thoughts. Whitman appeared slightly agitated, as if wanting to continue in the vein he had opened. Twain studied his cigar for a bit. Suddenly there were things going on under the surface of the conversation that I could not quite grasp.

"May I ask," Taylor began, speaking to me, "what you hope to uncover, or settle, in tomorrow's program?"

I thought about the words for a moment before answering. I had not thought of the conference in terms of "settling" anything, which phrase had odd overtones of terms of surrender. And the idea of "uncovering" something was . . . unanticipated. I had thought of the issues and topics as being somehow manifest in these men's and women's writings, and that what was wanted was a reaffirmation of the seriousness of the questions themselves, and perhaps a reordering of the relations among those questions. So I made a response more or less to that effect.

"So," Taylor said, "a dusting off of questions that have fallen into disuse. The questions themselves being the point. Am I hearing you correctly?"

"That's a way of putting it," I said. Something about his tone seemed designed always to put one on the defensive.

"It is *your* way of putting it," he said.

Twain cleared his throat and said, "Walt, I heard you were bringing out another edition of *Leaves of Grass*."

Whitman ignored the remark and said, "Questions! We want questions. Things are 'settled' only on tombstones!"

"And many settled 'things' are buried beneath," Taylor said, "with and without markers, and with wounds through which questions seep insistently into the nearby soil. The motives for exhumation should always be examined, would you agree?"

"I sat with the men in hospital for many days during the war years, Forrest," Whitman said. "Not those fortunate ones who died in battle but those with suppurating wounds and amputations, men of all aspect and from the Northern and Southern states alike, suffering beyond measure. I wrote letters for them. . . ."

"I would petition to allow them their rest in honor," Taylor said. "And glory, if I may say as much. By which I mean to ask what your intention was, sir,"—he was addressing me—"in placing me in direct conversation with Douglass on tomorrow's panel?"

"Come on, Forrest," Twain said. "Let's refill your glass and hear. . . ."

"I mean no disrespect to our host," he said. "Please believe me.

I truly want to find out his answer, only so that I might be able to focus my mind on the questions he expects to see addressed."

Now all three men regarded me, in anticipation of my answer, as one might await the next move in a chess game. I did not enjoy being placed in this position, and yet at one and the same time, I recognized that some adequate response was required. The brandy was serving both to loosen the constraints on any inhibition I might have had and to present certain challenges to the organization of what I had begun to think of as my mental troops. Taylor, I realized, had militarized my mind.

"I was born just before the war," I said, "and so have no direct or personal memory of it. I recognize that there were many factors contributing to it. But am I right at least in saying that for both sides it was a war fought in the name of freedom? In the North, for the sake of the freedom of the enslaved, as a way of approaching the ideals of freedom and human dignity for which the Revolutionary War was fought. And in the South for freedom to conduct the business within the respective states that those states perceived as being guaranteed them under the Constitution, without interference from an overreaching federal authority."

"The second part of your précis is accurate, as far as it goes," Taylor responded, "with the slight but significant emendation that our Revolutionary War was fought over the question of unjust taxation, not an abstract ideal of freedom. But your résumé of the Northern motivation in our late war is a very common and, if I may say, self-flattering view held in the North, and stoked by the abolitionists. The North did not expend its resources and waste the lives of tens of thousands of young men, as well as hundreds of thousands on the Confederate side, out of altruism. The late war was fought, on the Confederate side, as a means—a last resort, to use the phrase—of freeing the Southern states from intolerable constraints of trade placed upon us by the Northern states—unjust and tyrannical, as if we were a colony of the North. And on the question of 'freedom,' no one north of Baltimore had heard of the 'plight of the Negro,' or given it any thought until the abolitionist fever took hold and gave rhetorical sanction to the greatest act of mass piracy and tyrannical annexation that has ever taken place in human history. It was a matter of cold calculation, dressed up in the guise of solicitude for the Negro. And you may see just how abiding that concern is, now that the North's vanity and self-regard has been salved. They have quite abandoned any concern for the Negro now that the financial arrangements have been settled to their satisfaction."

These words, delivered with such force and eloquence, by nothing less than a general of the Confederacy, were daunting, to say the least, and I felt like Job quaking at the voice of the Lord. He had commanded thousands of men in battle, traveled throughout the country, participated in history. I noticed Twain watching me, as if to catch me should I fall. But despite a degree of fear—no other word for it—Taylor's words, or perhaps the tone in which they were delivered, activated some regiments of resistance within me.

"I can't pretend," I said, "that I am an expert in economics, or even much acquainted with it. Or them, I should say. Is it singular or plural?" I looked to Twain.

"I think it is a term of convenience for a field of study," he said, "and hence an aggregate, to be treated as a singular. Maybe best to say 'with the subject.' Carry on."

"The subject of economics, then. But supposing all you say is true, which I have to defer to you in the subject of." Brandy was doing its work; I would tighten up. "Given that the economic concerns drove all, as you say, what do you suppose the motives were of the abolitionists whom you allege to have fomented all this conflict? You say their rhetoric existed only to camouflage for Northern greed, yet for the abolitionist cause it was a serious question on its own terms, a spiritual question. . . ." I paused, gathered myself again. "And it seems to me that you also leave out the testimony of the former slaves themselves, which was certainly some part of my wish to place you in proximity to Frederick Douglass."

"Ah!" Taylor said. "And the famous horse of Troy is maneuvered, finally, into position. I assume that by 'the testimony of former slaves' you mean the well-rewarded rantings of Douglass and his ilk. How else, indeed, would he finance his acquisition of such well-tailored clothes, and the acquaintance of well-endowed Caucasian women. . . ."

"All right, Forrest," Twain said. "Can we . . ."

"Why wonder at it," Taylor went on, ignoring Twain. "The volumes of 'testimony,' as you call it. Enrichment, prominence, the desire to place oneself on the same footing with the white man. I see no mystery here."

"General Taylor," I said, struggling to keep my voice under control, "I am trying to answer your question in good faith, and I do not appreciate being placed under an artillery barrage! I do not—"

But I was interrupted by applause from Whitman, and one or two whistles from him, and a large, merry smile on Twain's face as he said, "Hear, hear!" The brandy had been working on all of us. And I even made out what I took to be a good-natured smile on Taylor's lips, accompanied by a slight bow of the head.

"Please," I went on, "all I mean to say is that I wanted to place individuals of eloquence in proximity and give them the opportunity to state their views so that they may stand out in contrast, and we might all learn by that contrast. That is what I meant to say."

"Splendid!" Twain said. "Well said! More brandy all around!" At this, Whitman held out his glass, which Twain refreshed, slightly.

"Yes," Taylor said. "These are questions which stir the emotions, and I apologize sincerely if I have abused your hospitality. We will have a vigorous and sincere exchange of ideas tomorrow, as you wish."

"I have a question," Whitman said. I saw Twain maintain the smile on his face as his eyes grew watchful, displeased. "Tomorrow will be an afternoon meant to address the question of the nature of freedom, among other things. Am I right about this?" He looked from face to face.

"Yes," I said.

"Do you propose to define the word in advance? Its meaning is elusive."

"I thought I would pose that as a task for each of the panelists in turn, to propose their own answers."

"Ah," Whitman said. "I'll have something to consider as I lie quite *freely* in my solitary bed this night." He was smiling at me. Twain, as one might expect, took the cue.

"And on that topic, gentlemen," he said, standing up, "we may all agree. Let us retire so that we may sustain the illusion, tomorrow, of our storied eloquence."

We all said good night cordially; Twain and Whitman headed upstairs to their respective rooms, and Taylor walked outside with me, a surprise, as he had been assigned a room at Harmony House. The rain—on the evidence only a light shower—had let up, and it was once again a clear, starlit evening. Answering my question before I could ask it, he said, "I think I'll go for a walk to clear my head a bit. Please believe that I meant no disrespect or harm. I am sorry if my words had too sharp an edge."

"Thank you," I said. "It is all well. Have a good walk."

"Yes, you too," he said, and started down Genesee Street toward town.

Back in my rooms I lay awake, my head afloat in the night's brandy. What had the day amounted to? Fragments . . . pieces here and there; none of it fit together. . . . American writers were unable to share a dais for an hour without practically coming to blows. . . . America . . . I threw the word around, but what did it mean? It was one thing to sing the principle of diversity, the fruitful tension among the parts, like Whitman, and quite another to face the insoluble contradictions, the ineradicable fact of the irrational, like Melville. One thing to be a social prophet, like Mrs. Stowe, and another to be an entertainer, like Lucy Comstock . . . Frederick Douglass, Forrest Taylor, Twain and his banjo player. . . . Something was just outside my grasp; I could hear it moving out there. . . . Horses pulling in different directions . . . Where was the *unum* of the *pluribus*? I imagined our Eagle swooping down like a vulture, the blood-stained beak, the greasy red-white-and-blue feathers . . . it perched on my leg and gnawed at my liver, as it had the day before, and the day before that. . . . The room turned like the stars in their courses, and I went to sleep with my clothes on.

— III —

– 11 –

THE OVERNIGHT RAIN had washed the downtown bricks, the damp morning sidewalks steamed, and the sun slowly dried the green and orange shop awnings. Saturday morning strollers stepped out to buy the paper, took the baby for a walk, performed errands at the market as the day warmed. Late in the morning, boats crisscrossed the lake, and at lunchtime picnickers lolled on the grassy banks.

A crowd began to fill Midlake Auditorium half an hour before the two o'clock start of the day's program. Word had spread that the event was free of charge, and first the ground-floor seats, then the balcony, then the aisles, and finally the lobby as well were crowded so that the doors into the auditorium were left open to afford the latecomers a view of the proceedings.

On the stage an extra table had been set up to accommodate the full complement of speakers, and at five minutes before the hour the audience saw Mark Twain, Harriet Beecher Stowe, Walt Whitman, Forrest Taylor, Lucy Comstock, and, at the far end, Frederick Douglass, all seated in a row next to Frederick Matthews, who had awakened that morning in his previous night's clothes, with a bad hangover and urgency riding his dreams.

After the encounter with Forrest Taylor, the morning offered a cold reckoning. He had envisioned a conversation, he realized, among books, not among the people who wrote them. What had he hoped for from these men and women, each of whom was some uneasy marriage between the public assertion and the private doubt, the completion achieved in each book and the inevitable fragmentary nature of the thought of any moment, each with an individual style that was impossible to submerge or dissolve in a collective vision? What was his hope, really, for the conference? What had he been trying to do? Whatever it was, the afternoon's session would be his last chance to do it.

Hangover or no hangover, he had set to work revising the remarks with which he hoped to frame the day's discussion. He worked until it was nearly time, fairly ran to Midlake, and found that Miss Pound's sister had not shown up, and the admissions table was not staffed. Once again, there was nothing to be done about it; there would be consequences, they would be faced, but later. . . . He found the writers, some of whom were in the lobby signing books, some lingering on the fringes of the auditorium, and herded them toward the dais.

Just as he reached the steps and was about to follow them to the stage, a young woman with dark red hair approached him, saying, "Sir—I wish you to have this." She was holding out a tiny envelope. "They are transit papers," she said. "You have won my affection." Matthews, puzzled, frowned, accepted it, and the woman turned and walked quickly away. On the front of the envelope was written only the word *Mockingbird*, in a loosely scrawled hand. Matthews stared at it for a moment, then jammed the envelope in his jacket pocket and mounted the stage.

The audience was a hive of conversations and greetings shouted and murmured. In those faces, one might have read a recognition of the unique moment, the historic import, the presence of legendary figures gathered onstage to call the nation to account and offer a guide to the future. Or was it only anticipation of entertainment, of a show, of men and women playing parts onstage until the curtain was lowered and the audience proceeded toward dinner, or the carnival, or a game of cards? The crowd was more diverse than it had been the day before; many had been at work then, but they came now. Men well turned-out in suits, men in serviceable jackets and vests and bowler hats, ladies in cloth gowns and some in satin. Some sat quietly, waiting for the program to begin; many spoke cordially with neighbors or others familiar from the town, and some looked around impatiently; a line of women in the seventh row held signs demanding women's votes, and several men in rough clothes looked up at the stage as if sizing up an opposing team. Three rowdies near the rear, who had clearly enjoyed a celebratory luncheon, laughed loudly and repeatedly, and drew disapproving glances. Wickham Moreland and a dozen business leaders and their wives had secured the front rows. Moreland had convinced them that the conference was a signal event in the evolution of Auburn as a center for business, one that would add luster to its reputation and attract investment. People arranged themselves so that they could attend to the proceedings in as much comfort as possible, given the now-crowded space, amid the fizz of anticipation.

As the hour approached, one dais seat was still vacant, and its intended occupant entered the auditorium only two minutes before the session was to commence. Herman Melville had been up since just after dawn, having begun work on a new story. The fever of the night before had somehow launched him, and he awoke with springtime in his heart. The salt air of possibility, a fresh voyage . . . he had felt his luck return, and he had rejoined himself. Upon entering the hall he paused to regard the figures assembled at the dais. Each had staked a claim to his own vision of the nation. Mark Twain, Frederick Douglass, Walt Whitman . . . Ambassadors, he thought, from Twain's America, Douglass's America, Whitman's

America. Each name a façade that, doubtless, people mistook for the man behind it. The mask donned, the face presented, the role assumed, the part played, as surely as Jack or John played Mr. Tambo or Mr. Bones. Pleased with the irony, he made his way up to the dais, where Matthews greeted him with relief.

At two p.m., with the dais complete and the hall full to overflowing, Matthews called the house to order. When the room had quieted he welcomed the crowd, and after formal remarks of introduction he began reading from his prepared text.

"What," he began, "is an American? This question might be answered differently at every hour of the day, on any street corner, by every person seated around any dinner table. The question is in fact a riddle. That it insists upon being asked may be, in itself, a clue to a response.

"At crucial times in our history, the question comes to the foreground. The question was first posed at the time of our Revolution, then during the writing of our Constitution, during the debates over slavery and the relations between states, and, most tragically and painfully, during our Civil War, when the very existence of the term hung in the balance.

"Now, weary with sacrifice, weary with grief, the nation has left the question alone to fend for itself, and like an untended garden covered with vines, its outlines have become obscured. We see the decoration and not the architecture, the surface and not the conflicted truth underneath, the promise of wealth without the reckoning of the debt.

"*What, finally, is America?* Our Civil War was fought to settle that question, and it is not settled yet. Perhaps it is not susceptible of final settlement. How, under such ambiguous conditions, can we move forward and create what the Founders called a 'more perfect Union'? How do we fulfill the responsibility that comes with the freedom we have paid for with blood and tears? This is the question—these, I should say, are the questions—which I want our distinguished panelists to address. In their books, these writers have offered their own versions of a response, their respective points of view. Yet no one vision can capture the entirety, and our hope today is that the *tension* among these visions might reveal something that each one, on its own, might illuminate only in part. And that together we might discover the outlines of a greater future. I have asked each panelist to offer some brief opening remarks, and I will ask Mr. Twain to begin."

A robust round of applause followed, and before Twain stood to acknowledge the audience he leaned over toward Matthews and said, "Nice job. My compliments," and then, patting his breast pocket, whispered, "I have the hair of the dog if you need it." Then he stood, nodded to the crowd, and smiled.

"Thank you," he said, as the ovation began to quiet. "Thank you very much. Your appreciation would have been impressive even had it not been amplified by the after-effects of the brandy I drank last night in the company of several of the gentlemen with whom I am sharing this stage. I am glad I survived to participate this afternoon.

"I have once again been asked to fire the starting pistol, this time on a discussion of the future of our nation. Although my years of experience as an after-dinner speaker have stood me in good stead this week-end, I have had very little experience as a clairvoyant, despite the opportunities for profit currently abounding in the spiritualist movement. I can communicate with neither the dead nor the unborn, let alone with historical figures of the future, and it is a considerable challenge to be asked to predict their activities. I have been known, however, on occasion to hazard a guess as to the likely performance of certain racehorses based upon proven records of past performance. So I will do my best to answer our host's questions, and perhaps some future handicapper may find my remarks useful.

"Among all the many and varied strengths and talents that have enriched our nation, the only one that rivals our aptitude for making money is the faculty of forgetting. In this I believe that America outpaces the entire world, and if a competition were held I doubt that any other country would dare challenge us. Unburdening oneself of inconvenient memories is one of the surest ways of making speed. Loyalty, indebtedness, lessons of past mistakes are but the pebbles in the shoes of a country on the make. The word 'Liberty' appears on our coinage, and I submit that we may wish to consider replacing it with the word 'Amnesia.'

"It is certainly true that we are living in a Golden Age of shameless ostentation. It is one of the sure signs that a nation is in the market for an Empire. If our Mexican War wasn't enough to convince you of this, stick around and we'll see what's down the road. In any case, if past performance is to be credited, the ruins of our Empire will, like the glories of the Classical world, draw gasps of appreciation and wonder in some museum of the future. In the meantime, the writer's responsibility consists in being faithful to what he sees and hears, even when he is imagining things. Maybe especially then. You can't falsify the evidence. That's the writer's morality. People are good and bad in varying proportions, and if the writer paints characters in monochrome he might as well draw stick figures. Thank you."

As it had been the previous afternoon, the audience throughout the hall was delighted by Twain's words. The essential grimness of his remarks passed unnoticed in the light of his wit and charm, and he was rewarded with great applause.

Frederick Matthews then asked Walt Whitman to speak.

Whitman's slouch hat of the day before was gone, along with the raffish, boulevardier light it had lent to his aspect, and his bald head and grey beard now seemed a reflection of his mood, which was autumnal as he stood and thanked the attendees for their applause.

"I am an old man now," he began, "and if I made any prediction for the future I wouldn't live to see if I was right or wrong. When I was young I believed that the words of a poet, free-minded, open, could influence the course of events. I don't think that's true now. You can change one reader's heart at a time, maybe, and that isn't nothing. Maybe it's everything. And you don't know where the seeds you sow are going to land.

"Here's what I think, anyway. America has a chance. It has a chance in principle. I don't believe there has ever been a society that has started with more hope, or greater ideals. No nation has ever tried to make such variant possibilities cohabit under one flag. The energies of the Virginia planter, the Downeaster on his lobster boat, the deer hunter, the riverboat strongback, the theater habitué of New York's Bowery, and the California gold prospector, gathered and seen together, are a new thing on the Earth. American by virtue of their shared idea. That's the idea behind Union in the first place.

"In principle. As I say, I am no longer young enough to think greed is going to be wiped out, or jealousy, or self-interest. I'm also old enough to know that people can change. Maybe not all the way around, but enough so that they can do better, see clearer. We have had our Civil War, and we are nearly twenty years into our chance at a new start. If the only lesson we learn is that we'd better not fight because it's bad for business, those lives were wasted. It is a bitter thing to say, because I sat with many young men in the hospitals, writing letters for them, hearing their dying moans. It would be tragedy upon tragedy to think that all of it happened and we learned nothing."

He looked down at the dais table for a long moment.

"I also want to say this. Nobody knows where electricity comes from, but when you have felt it you know that it is present. When you shake a man's hand, if you kiss a friend, or stranger, or say a comforting word, you complete a circuit. Seeing ourselves in another is the closest we come to Divinity. Nothing that raises that electricity is wrong, or shameful. Only the denying is shameful. What is done in passion may be forgiven—so say the courts, and so says the spirit. What is done in cold calculation may not be. I am sorry for my harsh words toward Herman Melville yesterday, and I offer my apologies to him. They were said in passion—misdirected and ill-considered—and I hope that I might be forgiven. Likewise if I have offended anyone at any point. I am an old man, as I have said. I have learned that some ways cannot be changed, but I have also learned that there are ways to make amends for mistakes that could not be helped. And I know we're supposed to be talking about America, and I am talking, again, about myself. But we are America, and maybe the future depends on making amends. Completing the circuit. Anyway, that's what I have to say."

Attendees were still arriving, pushing their way into the hall even as Whitman was acknowledging the applause. Just outside the lobby doors, people jostled one another for a view of the stage.

It was Mrs. Stowe's turn to speak.

"I'm not sure what I'm doing up here," she began. "I think I said that yesterday. What Whitman just said is probably as close to the root of any of this as you could get. What he calls Divinity somebody else might call the Holy Ghost. He leaves Jesus out of the picture, but so do a lot of people who throw our Lord's name around and act like they never heard a word He said. I think Whitman got the message either way.

"Slavery was a wound in our relation to Divinity. I didn't consider slavery a political issue, except as it needed to be solved by political means. Questions of justice, fairness, liberty, and so on—these have their foundation not in an ideal of society, but in the teachings and example of our Lord, to whom we owe the ultimate responsibility. These form the basis of all morality, and all governments are but servants of the welfare of the human beings who live under them. Or they ought to be. But I don't know that writers have any more responsibility to act according to those rules, or participate in the way society administers them, than anybody else does.

"By now it's tiresome to have to repeat the same old thing: Men—and women, alike—are entirely capable of attending church, making their offerings as if they could buy their way into Heaven or bribe God for a blessing, and then go out and treat human beings like farm animals to be bought, sold, and broken. If they see an incongruity in that, they've figured out a way to get around it. They'll be doing it for the next hundred years and the next thousand years.

"This is all obvious, and I don't know why I am sitting here. I said what I have to say in *Uncle Tom's Cabin*. People who didn't want to hear it started saying I had made up the brutality. So I put together a book with documentation, and now I keep writing books to keep expenses paid. That's what I've got to say."

As she sat down to mild applause, Frederick Douglass caught her eye and directed a smile and a nod in her direction, and Mrs. Stowe smiled, in return, for the first time that morning.

Herman Melville had sat looking out over the audience as he took in Mrs. Stowe's words. When he heard Matthews say his name, he stood to deliver his remarks.

"I should start by offering my thanks to Mr. Whitman for his words earlier," he began, and bowed toward the poet. "Certainly he was no more at fault than I. Often one finds that opposites have more in common than they appear to, and more, even, than close neighbors. In any case, I thank you."

Whitman closed his eyes and nodded toward Melville.

"In truth," Melville went on, "I see a kinship, distinguished not so much in the substance of our perceptions, but perhaps in the conclusions drawn therefrom. Or perhaps not the conclusions but rather the mood elicited by those perceptions. We both perceive a vastness, an expanse. I believe that he sees the expanse as a gallery of possibilities in endless combination, a polyphony of regions, interests, aptitudes, and so forth. The vast continent is his whaling ship, perhaps, and my *Pequod* a continent of its own. Forgive me if I am simplifying your words beyond recognition. . . ."

"Go on," Whitman said. "I am interested."

"Whether on land or on the sea, discovery, exploration, sometimes possibility itself, seems somehow wedded to the wish to dominate, subdue, and control. Yet even the New World must come to a terminus. Something there is in the American makeup that is enraged by limitation. The restlessness, the acquisitive fever to which Mr. Twain addressed himself . . . that restless expansion is fueled by something that ignites into rage when blocked in any way. And enraged not by the blockage alone, but by the unknowability of what lies beneath, the unreadable intent that appears to be malice. Is there in fact a malevolent intent, or merely an inner persecutor, projected outward? When that malevolence, embodied, meets goodness, is such goodness a projection as well?

"Is there any comfort to be gained in the fact that this pattern has been repeated down the ages? The same hungers, the same illusions and mistakes, the same glories and the same tragic outcomes? Writers may write of love and reunion, or they might depict the wreck of thousands of lives, but if they are writing well they are equally happy. And if they are unable to write they will be miserable even in Paradise. Thank you."

Puzzled applause. A shaft of afternoon sunlight now shone through the balcony's rear window, and the air throughout the hall grew warmer; ladies fanned themselves here and there. Frederick Douglass and Forrest Taylor sat quietly, avoiding any acknowledgment of one another. Frederick Matthews introduced Lucy Comstock, who received a response surpassing even the ovation she had received the day before.

"Thank you," she said. "I hope I won't appear trivial after all these profound words if I say that I think the main responsibility of a writer is to entertain one's readers. We are bedeviled enough in our day-to-day lives without having to sink deeper into gloom when we open a book. I am aware, as we noted yesterday, that the lives of women and the affairs of the heart may seem frivolous to some—little cottages next to the cathedrals and battlefields of so-called serious literature. Yet I would say that the events and complications in those little cottages are quite as significant as these large themes, if not more so. The future of America is quite capable of taking care of itself, and to ask the seamstress, the cook, and the nursemaid to take responsibility for the workings of an entire continent and many thousands of souls seems somewhat unrealistic to me. Most people do not dwell in a dreamland of large themes, and they want to see their own lives—insignificant as those lives may appear to certain writers—reflected in a book they might find time to pick up."

"Miss Comstock," Twain said, playfully, "I thought I heard you say that books ought to be an escape. It sounds like you're saying they should set the reader right back down in the lives they're trying to escape."

"Mr. Twain, I don't mean that one should force a woman to

read about the laundry, the drudgery, the hundred little demerits that might accrue to her account each day if she isn't a dutiful wife. I mean rather that the passions that every woman will recognize, the desires, and the possibilities, all of which are so often foreclosed to her when she assumes the role of wife and mother, are a fit means of restoring some degree of spirit. Does that mean nothing to you? You write so movingly about childhood—is this not a similar vein?"

"Maybe it is," Twain said. "Maybe it is."

"And, too," Miss Comstock went on, "why is it important to make these distinctions among different kinds of writers? We are all writers—aren't we all contributing something of value? Who is to say that a few hours' escape from a dreary day isn't every bit as valuable as some ponderous philosophical diatribe?"

"What's wrong with making distinctions?" Mrs. Stowe said.

"I simply don't see why it is necessary to create hierarchy," Miss Comstock said, turning toward her. "Whom does it serve? Whom does it exclude?"

"You speak as if it's imposed," Mrs. Stowe said. "It's not imposed; it's evident on the face of things. Anybody with a brain knows there are different degrees of talent. I would never think of measuring myself against Shakespeare, or Dickens."

Twain stepped in, saying, "Maybe it's not a hierarchy; maybe it's just a difference. Writers aim for different things. One person likes pineapples and the other likes oranges. They're both good, but that doesn't mean they are one big pineorange."

The audience laughed at this.

Matthews saw this as the moment to step in, and he thanked Lucy Comstock and was about to introduce Forrest Taylor when there was a commotion in the audience and someone shouted, "I demand to speak!"

– 12 –

MARGARET LEWIS STANFORD had risen to her feet.

"We have endured this asinine blather long enough," she said. "The most pressing question of our time—that of women's suffrage—is about to be consigned once again to the margins of a conversation that is supposedly about the future of the nation— a future that will not exist without the participation of women."

"Madam—" Matthews began.

"I am not Madam—you know my name by now. We will not be the caboose on this train. Are we invisible, indeed? Along with my sisters, I find myself—ourselves—asked once again to move to the end of the line, asked to wait until others have had their say on the more 'urgent' questions under discussion. This afternoon we will not be the dessert; we will be a full constituent of the main course. If need be we will upset the entire table in the name of simple justice."

A man shouted, "Sit down and let's get on with it!"

"I will sit down when I am ready, and when I am finished with what I have to say."

Cheers, a few catcalls.

"The advancement of justice and opportunity depends upon the making and administering of the law. Despite the demurrals we hear from Miss Comstock, who is smart enough to know better, women are every bit as capable of discharging that responsibility as men—if not more so! Those who write the law are exclusively men, and those who decide which men shall write the law are men, exclusively, as well. How may any sensible person justify denying to woman, to half the population, a voice in these decisions, and an equal hand in the making of that law? Why was no representative of the women's movement invited to a place on this panel alongside Mr. Douglass? A war was fought for the freedom of the Negro, and the Negro has had the franchise these past fourteen years, while women yet await the enacting into law of a right which should have been ours long ago. How is that justice? I say let us fight! Women will have the vote, and women will have a voice!"

At this, the eight women to Mrs. Stanford's immediate left stood, cheered, and held up signs reading *VOTES FOR WOMEN*. A few shouted remarks greeted the demonstration, as well—"Tell the harridan to sit down!" "Let her speak!" "Where's your umbrella?"

It was Frederick Douglass who stilled the crowd by standing and asking, "May I respond to my friend Mrs. Stanford?

"If I may speak," he began. "I have been an advocate of women's suffrage from the very beginning, as Mrs. Stanford well knows. We have stood shoulder to shoulder literally as well as figuratively, since the Seneca Falls convention and before. On one issue alone have we found ourselves on opposing sides of a question—whether to advance first, and primarily, the cause of women's suffrage, or the right of the Negro to vote. No decent person can justify denying the right of the franchise to members of any group; the question at that time was one of urgency, of which group was in more immediate need of the relief that only a change in the law could bring about. I have always been a women's suffrage man, and shall continue to lend my efforts and my voice to women's struggle for equality." He nodded to Mrs. Stanford and sat down.

Mrs. Stanford, still standing, responded. "With all respect to Mr. Douglass, it is only fair to point out that the situation of women begged for redress long before the situation of the Southern Negro. Yet when the question of suffrage came to the crisis in the aftermath of the war, it was argued—successfully, in the issue—that it would be easier to enlist public sentiment to give the Negro the franchise than to extend that franchise to the Woman who makes up fully half the population, and the Negro was granted his right to vote with the Fifteenth Amendment to the Constitution. I should say, to be more precise, the Negro *male* was granted this right. Women, no matter their color, were, and are, deemed too fragile, too necessary for housework and childbearing, to be trusted with a say in the affairs of the world—which affairs surely bear down at least as heavily upon women as upon the male population!"

Applause.

"And, indeed," she went on, "while supporting fully the right of all human beings to have a say in their fate, we asked why people who in most cases could neither read nor write, who knew nothing of history or culture, were given precedence at the expense of educated women every bit as capable of reading a newspaper as their husbands, every bit as capable of writing a law, or composing a symphony. The Negro needs to be brought along, blended into our society, but this is not something that can happen with the stroke of a pen granting them the vote."

Douglass had retaken his seat, but now, clearly annoyed, he rose and said, "I do not wish to extend this argument, but in fairness I must object to this characterization of the men—and women—of my race. I will repeat now what I said fifteen years ago when this question was still a live nerve in our discourse—'When women, because they are women, are hunted down in the cities of New York and New Orleans; when they are dragged from their houses and are hung from lamp-posts; when their children are torn from their arms, and their brains bashed out upon the pavement . . . then they will have an urgency to obtain the ballot equal to our own.' And I will add that even today, *with* the franchise, the Negro— whether common laborer, doctor, or professor—too often exercises his Constitutional right to vote at the price of his life! Thank you." And he sat again. Cheers from isolated pockets of the audience, silence from others.

"And to that," Mrs. Stanford shouted, "I reply that no one has disputed that the Negro has been mistreated. So have the Irishman, the Chinee, and the Indian. But let the educated woman lead the way! In the words of Elizabeth Cady Stanton—'To claim that Patrick and Sambo and Yung Tung, who don't know the difference between a monarchy and a republic, who never read the Declaration of Independence, deserve the franchise in front of the women who educate men's children and maintain their households, is to degrade your own mothers, wives, and daughters below unwashed and unlettered ditch-diggers, boot-blacks, butchers, and barbers!'"

Mrs. Stowe, scandalized, cried out, "For God's sake!" Shouts reverberated now from every corner of the hall. Lucy Comstock, two seats away, was applauding, and much of the audience seemed stunned by the sudden turn the conversation had taken, none more than Matthews himself, who called out in exasperation, "Please! This argument was settled with the passing of the Fifteenth Amendment, and we all agree that women should have the franchise."

"No we don't!" cried a voice from the audience, followed by more shouting.

"*I am the moderator*," Matthews said, slapping the dais table, "and I will be forced to close this session if civility is not the rule."

Whitman shouted, "Hear, hear!" Cries from the audience— "Yes!" "Everyone be quiet!"

"I have asked the members of the panel to speak," Matthews went on. "We will have open discussion later. Will you agree to that?"

Widespread assent.

"Then we may proceed. I now invite General Forrest Taylor to offer his opening remarks."

Matthews gave a brief introduction, after which Taylor stood at his place and received a round of polite applause.

"I will admit," he began, "to being both surprised and gratified by the invitation to participate in this conference, the goal of which, as I understand it, is to bring together divergent points of view in the hopes of setting aside former grievances and forging a common future. This is a goal devoutly held in view by men of good will—and women," he added, with a courtly bow, "from the North and South alike, in the process of aspiring to which we may all find our differences not nearly so great as our common interests. As a general of the Confederacy I have seen at first hand the costs in life and livelihood exacted by the attempt to enforce the interests of one section upon the interests of another. It is the promise of our day that a more just and equitable arrangement shall obtain, in the interests of the greatest benefit for all."

Frederick Matthews sat listening to these words, wondering what had happened to Taylor's scalding sarcasm and anger of the night before. Had the general undergone a religious conversion in his sleep? Was there any other way of understanding the conciliatory tone and content of his remarks?

"As the South seeks to reconstruct *itself*," Taylor went on, "it welcomes the hand of friendship from those in the North who recognize our common interest and share in an understanding that the South can, and must, restore an order that has been violated not so much by a war—which we lost in the face of overwhelming manpower and resources—but by the imposition of the subsequent restrictions intended to dismantle a system that had existed since well before the nation itself came into being. The withdrawal of the last federal troops from the Southern states has gone some good distance toward correcting the excesses of Reconstruction, so-called, which might with more justice have been termed 'Institutional *De*struction.' It signals the recognition—late, yes, but to be welcomed—that the traditions of many generations may not be summarily demolished without causing great anguish and discord.

"There are some who still at this late hour see a profit in stoking the dying embers of discord. Yet even as we speak, efforts move forward to restore the sense of pride among a soldiery, and a populace, that gave the last full measure, to quote a phrase, of their blood and toil in a Cause they believed to be just. It is my hope that all men of good will might cheer this as a true sign of the reconciliation for which we strive. And in the near future we may hope to see the hand of friendship and mutual interest extended across the Mason-Dixon Line, among the men who fought in this most costly and tragic war on both sides—to join together and move forward, unencumbered by the sectional, nay factional, distractions that led to our war."

These concluding words elicited a nearly universal assent. On the dais, Mark Twain, Lucy Comstock, and even Walt Whitman applauded—How indeed, their expressions seemed to say, could one help but cheer reunion, forgiveness, common cause, and progress? Yet while the others applauded, Harriet Beecher Stowe and Herman Melville both sat silently: Stowe with an exasperated frown, and Melville with an expression that was part recognition, part amusement, and part resignation.

Frederick Douglass had sat listening impassively and seemed almost, at times, lost in thought. When he heard Matthews mention his name by way of introduction, he smiled and stood to the largest ovation of the day. After ten seconds he raised his hand and thanked everyone for the reception.

"I wish to begin," he said, "with an apology to my longtime ally Mrs. Stanford, for the heat of some of my earlier remarks. We have known one another for many years, and while we have had disagreements at times over tactics, and even strategy, we have always been in harmony as to the ultimate goals of freedom and universal participation in our democracy. I salute you, Mrs. Stanford."

Mrs. Stanford, seated in the seventh row, nodded and saluted him in return, and the audience, especially the suffragists, clapped their approval.

"I will make an admission of my own," he went on, "at the outset of my remarks. It is an admission to a degree of confusion, or perhaps wariness, at the stated theme of this concluding session: *The Future of America*. At first blush it would appear to be the brightest of marks for which to steer. How, indeed, might a navigator make his way without a desired destination? And how, indeed, without a map of the shallows, the depths, and the hazards, all learned from experience? How approach a discussion of the future absent a reckoning with the past?

"Amnesia does seem to be a theme this afternoon. Mr. Taylor—forgive me—*General* Taylor—has advanced a most sanguine and optimistic vision of a future in which the South and the North may not only resolve but forget their differences and join hands in mutual interest. The foot soldier, the cavalryman, the cannoneer are enjoined now to recognize their common lot, the war seen as a noble effort on both sides, and one out of which, certainly, both sides may, in the tradition of good sportsmanship and manly practicality, proclaim honor and move forward.

"In framing the situation in this manner for our audience, he has demonstrated his generalship skills, by mounting a kind of preemptive strike, attempting to claim the high ground of graciousness, rationality, and forward thinking for himself and his cause. This preemptive narrative, is, in fact, already in process of being constructed. The South has been busy imposing an entirely new set of memories upon the nation. No longer a mutinous cadre steered by traitors to the Union, but a gallant population fighting for an idyllic, even Edenic, way of life that was defeated in an epic contest, out of which came heroes whose legends may be burnished ever more brightly in the warm sunlight of memory. Even now they are erecting equestrian monuments to these exemplars of bravery, who will ride into bronze and marble glory in perpetuity along the boulevards of Richmond and the other capitals of the Confederacy. They are even, it appears, organizing reunions with their long-ago adversaries on the field of honor. This past April, in Luray, Virginia, there was instituted a Robert E. Lee camp dedicated to the Lost Cause, and there are plans for many more of these.

"Remarkable indeed that in the reenactments not one Negro soldier has been invited or acknowledged. How now? Why should this be? Where are the monuments to the Negro soldier and sailor, some two hundred thousand of whom served the cause of Union gallantly, and often at mortal cost? Where, for that matter, are the monuments to the bondsman forced to work the cotton and cane fields under the lash, whose labor formed the basis of the South's prosperity?

"The entire reason for the war was the insistence among the slave-holding interests that slavery be admitted to all prospective states and territories. I realize that the debates are now twenty-five and thirty years in the past, and may be difficult indeed for the resolutely future-minded to remember, but they hinged on nothing other than this.

"Why tear open these wounds, you ask? Why not let bygones be bygones? Are not the former Confederates honorable men? It were a reasonable question if that past did not bear down upon the colored population daily, with the honorable boots of the Confederacy on their neck. A reasonable question, except that these gallant cavaliers, these honorable paragons of a never-were nobility, will not let bygones be bygones; they wish nothing less than to restore the conditions that obtained before the war—Taylor has said it himself. And if that were not obtainable through legal means, it would be obtained through brute force. The Negro, you see, will not let him forget, because the Negro will not—cannot—disappear. And as long as he walks the Earth, he is an ever-present reproach to the former slaveholder, a burden on the Southern conscience—a reproach and a burden upon whom a vicious revenge must be enacted!

"Of course the former slaveholder wishes to forget, and to replace the bitter facts with a fairy tale of his own devising, so that we may all 'move forward.' And because he *cannot* forget, the past, present, and future alike are burned alive, mutilated, hanged upon trees in public squares and in Godforsaken forests. The truth itself is lynched, even as we speak. And in the interests of order, of progress, of commerce, of a disingenuous titular reconciliation, when the truth is charred beyond recognition and the honorable townspeople are satisfied, they will cut down the tree and paint the stump red, to remind those who need reminding of the price they will pay for remembering."

During these words a dozen or more audience members had risen to their feet, shouting assent and derision, at Douglass and Taylor alike, as well as at other audience members. Douglass sat down, and a tidal wave of shouts and applause, a clamor, angry and nearly impenetrable, washed through the room, and the other members of the panel now sat quietly, clearly uncertain as to what was to happen next. In the front rows, Moreland and his party looked stricken; Moreland was directing a pointed look at Matthews, who stood again at his seat and shouted, "Anyone shouting epithets will be ejected from the hall. These men and women will be heard with respect!"

A voice shouted, "This is a democracy!" A few turned in their seats and shouted at the disrupters to be seated.

In the front rows, Wickham Moreland and Amos Smith could be seen locked in conversation. After some moments, Moreland got Frederick Matthews's attention and pointed to Amos Smith emphatically several times, indicating that he wished for Smith to rise and address the gathering. Matthews nodded and was about to make the announcement when Amos Smith himself stood, turned to face the hall, and began speaking.

"Ladies and gentlemen—fellow citizens of Auburn," he began, "I know many of you, and for those I don't know, I'm Amos Smith. I'm the president of Cayuga Savings."

Smith was one of the town's wealthiest and most prominent citizens, a shopkeeper's son who had worked his way up and enjoyed advancing himself as an advertisement for civic possibility. The audience, recognizing him, did indeed quiet down considerably.

"This week-end's event has been a real feather in Auburn's cap," he said, "a sign that we are 'playing with the big boys,' as the saying goes. We're entering a new era of prosperity and prominence. This program tells everybody we aren't just a whistle stop between Buffalo and Albany. We are cultured, too, with the best of them. I know that there are a few reporters out there in the audience. Let's not send them to their desks with news of a lot of foolishness. How about a big hand for Mark Twain, Louise . . . Fred . . . the general . . . What'd I say? Lucy! Slip of the tongue . . . We have a whole lineup of famous writers up here, so let's listen to what they have to say, so everyone can go and spread the word that Auburn is open for business and ready for progress. Thank you."

He sat down as the citizens around him applauded, a few shouting, "Hear, hear!"

While Amos Smith was speaking, Matthews thought of a stratagem to regain control of the program and focus attention back upon the writers at the dais. After he had thanked the bank president, he quickly announced the next part of the program.

"We are here, as you know, to talk about our nation and its prospects. With a view toward that end, I would like to continue by asking each member of this panel to respond to the question I proposed at the outset of today's session: 'What is an American?' I know I have sprung this on you rather by surprise, but"—he looked down the line of the writers—"I would be interested to hear your thoughts. Mr. Twain?"

Twain shot Matthews a look that said "You're making me lead off again?" Then he spoke.

"I'd say an 'American' is somebody who can make his way in the greatest number of social settings. Or rather among the greatest diversity of company. The fellow who can be equally comfortable with a dockhand or a senator." Twain turned to his left and looked at Harriet Stowe.

"It's my turn?" Mrs. Stowe said. "I don't know. Somebody who lives in America. How about that? And accepts the responsibility that goes along with it." Her matter-of-fact delivery elicited some quiet appreciative laughter through the hall. In turn she looked to her left, at Whitman.

"I think I'm pretty close to Twain on this," Whitman said. "I'd say an American is somebody who feels himself kin to everyone. Not just feeling comfortable with them, but the spiritual kinship."

Melville, next in line, began, "I think of this question more as a request for the common thread than for a definition. I can't imagine a single word or phrase that could define an American, given the etymology of the word 'define,' indicating limits and ending. I would say that all Americans share responsibility for the fate of an unlikely social ideal. I think that is fair to say. You could also say that Americans all wear masks. Because as Americans, absent the history of centuries, we must needs invent our roles based on new factors, new landscapes . . . new proximities." Here he paused. "I suppose I haven't really answered the question, and I'll cede the floor and give it some further thought."

As Melville spoke, Lucy Comstock made her impatience evident, and when her turn arrived she said, "I think the answer is very simple: someone who enjoys the greatest freedom in the world, in the greatest country in the world."

Mrs. Stowe quickly responded, "Then the Negro isn't an American?"

"Oh, of course," Forrest Taylor broke in. "It always comes back to 'the Negroes.' They are free now, are they not? It will never be enough for them."

"Here!" Melville said, "I will amend my previous attempts. An American is one for whom there is no such thing as 'enough.'"

Everyone, except for Taylor, now looked to Frederick Douglass, who seemed, suddenly, very tired. He said, "An American is one who insists upon defining *himself*—who does not accept a definition imposed by others. Maybe ultimately one would say it is one who defines himself as 'an American.'"

Walt Whitman interjected, "I want to add that our diversity is the source of our strength and health! Our Constitution was written to recognize it and encourage it. The spirit in me is the spirit in you, and in all. Diversity is the divine in man and woman, the spirit of all in each individual, you and me . . . a principle of unity, not division."

"With all respect, Mr. Whitman," Forrest Taylor broke in, "the Constitution is an instrument designed to lay out an arrangement for freedom of trade, absent the constraints imposed by a distant monarchical power, and then to administer the benefits thereof. If this sounds at all like the motive behind the South's attempt at securing freedom for itself, perhaps it is no coincidence. It was intended to organize a society in which the varieties of interest might be negotiated with something approximating fairness. Virginia would not dictate to New York how to be New York; Boston would not dictate to Georgia. And so on. Such laws as were devised to address the challenges of a confederation among independent states with immense differences in resources and needs, were devised exactly thus. Not to rewrite the Bible or call down the millennium upon us. It is a civil document, not a religious tract, with all apologies to Mr. Whitman and Mrs. Stowe. And it is meant to be administered by men with some grasp of the way things work on Earth, not in Heaven, and not abolitionists and freethinkers who arrogate unto themselves a supposed knowledge of the Lord's intent."

"I don't know what the heck you're talking about," Harriet Stowe said. "The sole purpose of the United States Constitution was to allow you and your brigands to trade freely in slaves? This is the intent of the nation's founding? Have you ever read the Constitution? The freedom of speech, worship, assembly, the separation of powers, *habeas corpus* . . . these are all there to serve the interests of slave owners? How convenient!"

"What I mean to say is—"

"I'm not finished. Regarding 'the Lord's intent'—God's views, and those of His Son, are very clearly stated in the Bible, and everyone knows those words. It is not His fault that His words are twisted and made to seem to justify actions that will surely meet with judgment in the Afterlife. It's there in the Ten Commandments and in the Sermon on the Mount, and it was there when His Son asked forgiveness for His persecutors as He faced death on the Cross. . . ."

"It might also be argued, Ma'am," Taylor responded, "that there are some sins—or to use a less theologically charged term, *crimes*—which Man has no right to forgive. In whose name do we forgive mass slaughter, thievery, the subjugation of an entire populace for the sake only of gain, under the hypocritical claim of righteousness—"

"*Thank you!*" Frederick Douglass shouted. "Thank you for proclaiming your self-indictment with such clarity and moral force! Who, indeed, is the hypocrite? The South refuses to reckon with the consequences of its treachery—"

"Hypocrite?" Taylor said. "Was the South, indeed, allowed to dress its own wounds? To make that reckoning for itself? To find its path forward out of the errors of the past? Was it indeed? It was not. How, pray tell, should anyone robbed of their independence be held responsible for a reckoning with their own actions? Forced to bow and scrape, to watch wives and children starve while Northern troops raped their daughters and stole the meager food off their tables, and enforced the rule of ignorant former slaves who swung from the chandeliers in the Senate chambers of every Southern capitol . . ."

A chorus of boos and hoots arose, and a man in the rear of the hall shouted, "Then maybe you shouldn't have started the war!" This precipitated a more general shouting; people turned in their seats to see who was shouting what at whom; some were amused by the excitement, some were clearly frightened. Frederick Matthews's shouted demand for order was lost in the commotion. Someone in the back had exclaimed, "Freemasons control the government!"

A shabbily dressed man stood in the third row, jabbed his finger at Frederick Douglass, and said, "You think you're as good as a white man?"

"That," Douglass said, "would depend on the white man, wouldn't it?"

"What about me?" the questioner asked. "You think you're better than me?"

"How would I know?" Douglass said. "I don't know you."

A man seated in front of the questioner turned around in his seat and said, "Why don't you sit down, trash?"

"Who's trash, Bruder?"

"You know damned well," the man said.

The questioner leaned forward and struck the man on the side of the head. Several people cried out, and the seated man rose with difficulty in order to return the blow, as two men tried to restrain him. Voices from around the room called for them to stop, for someone to intervene; two or three hollered encouragement. Matthews summoned Lemuel Fowler from the side of the stage and directed him to leave the hall and find the police who had been stationed outside.

A voice was shouting, "You profane the Sabbath!"

"The Sabbath is the Seventh Day! Saturday is the Seventh Day!"

Something was coming apart in the room; a latch seemed to have sprung open and energies were being loosed, the advance guard of the irrational, a mutiny. . . . Matthews watched it, shocked by its suddenness. A bearded man three rows back rose to his feet and shouted, "Abraham Lincoln was a Jew!"

Laughter ricocheted through the hall.

"Ridiculous!"

"Sit down!"

"I *read* it," the man responded. "The Jews from France were behind him. The Rothmans."

A short man with red hair stood and shouted, "They were expelled from Atlantis! It's in Donnelly's book."

Two audience members had approached the stage and were yelling something at the panelists, inaudible now in the general din. They were joined almost immediately by Wickham Moreland, who tried to shoulder one of them aside, precipitating a shoving match. Voices from around the hall shouted agreement and disagreement, standing up, pointing fingers. And unnoticed by anyone, the man who called himself the Prophet Ben Hamouda had stood in the far aisle and raised his arms as if calling for attention.

"Ye have made a covenant with death!" he shouted.

Several dozen attendees were making their way toward the exits, which were largely blocked by the crowd outside pressing to gain entry. A dozen others made their way to the front of the auditorium and were shouting at the writers on stage, and at one another.

Margaret Lewis Stanford turned to her cohorts, gave a signal, and they rose as one and began singing:

> Mine eyes have seen the glory of the coming of the Lord,
> He is trampling out the vintage where the grapes of wrath
> are stored . . .

"A house without mortar!" the Prophet shouted. "A church without an altar! A grandfather without a memory! A plantation in the sky! Adultery! *Adulteration! Woe to the crown of pride!* Your agreement with hell *shall not stand. . . ."* At that moment a rock thrown by a man at the very rear of the hall and intended for someone else struck the Prophet in his temple, and the Prophet fell to one knee, screaming, *"Amanna bo shah holannah ba sho mannah . . ."*

The crowd at the edge of the stage had grown to more than thirty, pushing, and shouting; several Town Line citizens argued first with Douglass and Taylor, and then among themselves; that argument was joined by more audience members and in one convulsive push proceeded onto the stage itself, where the man named Bruder, the baker from Town Line, attempted to land a blow on Forrest Taylor, who stepped quickly out of the way, causing the baker's fist to land instead just above Mark Twain's eye. Mrs. Stowe, unaware of the assailant's Union sympathies, landed her own blow, a disabling kick to the baker's midsection. . . .

Five policemen arrived to quell the riot, and even with the aid of their nightsticks it took a full ten minutes to subdue the combatants. Before their arrival Walt Whitman had tried several times to intervene in individual skirmishes, but he succeeded only in getting himself pushed to the floor and bruising his hip. Melville pushed one of the drunken rowdies off the stage. Lucy Comstock had quit the dais as soon as the confrontation began and returned to the Owasco Hotel. Forrest Taylor, distracted by watching her leave, was caught unaware by a blow from the baker's assistant, Rolf by name, and sustained a mildly sprained shoulder. Frederick Douglass had taken especial care not to allow himself a physical engagement with any of the assailants, well aware that the weight of blame would fall on him despite his renown, and even, perhaps, because of it. Eventually, three more police arrived, and a dozen combatants were arrested and brought in two wagons to the Auburn Correctional Facility.

When the hostilities had been largely subdued, a reporter claiming to be from the New York *World* talked his way past the police and pestered Mark Twain (successfully) and several other participants (unsuccessfully) for a quotation he might use for an article. He did elicit a pithy quote from a janitor, and as he was about to leave he noticed Frederick Matthews, hiding behind a stage curtain and weeping. Mustering a solicitous expression, the reporter approached, but Matthews was able only to blurt out the words "Why did it have to end this way?"

–13–

SUNDAY MORNING dawned grey and damp. Church bells in the distance, the quiet streets.

At 9:30 a.m. a plate of baked ham sat, almost untouched, in front of Harriet Beecher Stowe at the train depot's counter. Next to her, Mark Twain wiped his mouth with his napkin and reached for his water glass.

"I do not think that young man is equipped for this work," Mrs. Stowe said. "I feel badly for him."

"He does appear to be in over his head," Twain responded. He pulled a pocket flask from inside his jacket, emptied his water glass into a nearby pitcher, and replaced the water with an inch of Scotch. "He stood up pretty well under a bombardment from Taylor the other night."

"Taylor's a bad piece of work. I can't see why he was invited."

"He's had a pretty tough row," Twain said. "His wife's in bad shape."

"I'm sorry for her, but he is a bad piece of work." Mrs. Stowe looked around the room. "What time are we boarding?"

"We have half an hour," Twain said.

They sat quietly for a few moments.

"I don't know what the hell this all amounted to," Twain said.

"I've said that all along," she said.

"Well," Twain said, suddenly irritable, "you sold some books, didn't you?"

"Mostly counterfeits from Philadelphia. You did well."

"I'm going home with a box," he said.

"You had fun Friday night."

"It was fun until it wasn't fun," he said. "Like everything else." He was quiet for a moment, then he said, "How's your ham?"

"Glorious," she said, flatly.

This made Twain laugh out loud, and his mood seemed to brighten on the instant. "I don't know what happened to poor old Walt with that poem Friday. He seemed fine yesterday."

Mrs. Stowe grunted. "Your friend did quite well for himself."

"Henry? Henry might be the one genius I have known in my lifetime."

"Douglass didn't seem to think much of him," she said.

"Douglass gave me a copy of the latest retelling of his life story," he said. "I gave him *Roughing It*." He took a long sip of the Scotch. "Two washerwomen taking in each other's laundry."

Across the room, she saw the red-haired girl she had glimpsed at Friday's lunch.

"I recognize that girl from somewhere," she said. "She's somebody's cousin, I think."

Twain, she noticed with some annoyance, seemed to have drifted off to his own planet. Likely figuring out a way to waste another few thousand dollars on some fool scheme.

As if to himself, Twain said, "*All right—I'll go to hell, then!*"

"What?" Stowe said, alarmed.

Twain seemed to float back to Earth, and he laughed at her shocked expression.

"I just wrote my epitaph," he said. "I might have to sand it down a little." Then he looked at himself in the mirror behind the counter, raised his glass in salute, and took a drink.

Mrs. Stowe grunted and shrugged. There's no fool, she thought to herself for the millionth time, like a damned fool.

———

"Good evening," said the tall, handsome man in the long jacket, which was draped raffishly over his shoulders.

"Good evening," Eliza replied, a flush coming to her cheeks. "Won't you come in?"

Lucy Comstock ate the last of her breakfast in her room at the Owasco Hotel as she read over the pages she had written. Cora was downstairs settling the bill at the desk and arranging for a carriage to take them to the station.

She had begun work that week-end on a new novel, which she had titled *The General's Lady*.

"I was surprised at your invitation," General Forrest Baylor said, stepping into the room.

"Is a surprise a bad thing?"

"Only in battle," the general replied, "and only when on the receiving end. May I?"

"Of course," she replied, taking his coat from him and laying it over the back of one of the brocaded French chairs placed around the elegant chamber. "It is my pleasure to make you as . . . comfortable as possible." She smiled coquettishly.

The general leaned back in the chair he had taken; a scar

**could be seen under his left ear. Relic of a heroic battle, she
had no doubt. His exploits were famed throughout the land.**

Late Saturday night, Forrest Taylor had in fact knocked on her
door, per their agreement earlier that day. Lucy had been more
than a little annoyed, as his lateness implied that he was in no
great hurry to visit her. His presence, however, was compelling—
his stature, his boots, the way he looked around the room, as if
taking ownership of it. It was, she realized, the same way she herself looked at any new person or situation. Taking ownership, for
later use in a book.

He had come, he said, from a drinking bout with Mark Twain
and the conference's host. He described the conversation to her,
asked a few desultory questions about her evening. After ten minutes of parlor chat, she wondered how long it would be before he
decided to get down to the business at hand.

"May I ask you something?" she had said, finally.

"You may ask me anything you like."

"Do you find me attractive?"

He was visibly taken aback by the question. After a moment,
he said, "Very."

"Did you have any intention of acting upon your perception this
evening?"

**The general rose from his chair and approached her. She
looked up into his face and imagined time disappearing,
and all of her life that had been so difficult, the thankless
work, the daily struggle, and she thought, yes, take me . . .**

take me. . . . She stood and looked into his eyes and smelled his musky cologne as his arms encircled her in the captivity she desired with every fiber of her being.

"Kiss me," she gasped.

And she felt his lips on hers, like the sun upon a waiting field wet with dew, her self disappeared, her will was his will. . . .

"I cannot," he said, breaking away.

This last line was drawn from life.

"What?" she had said. "Why?"

He stepped away.

"My wife," he said. "She is ill, and I have felt considerable doubt about making this trip to begin with, and this . . . this is a temptation to which I must not submit. I am sorry."

"Your wife," she said.

"Does it surprise you that I am married?"

"It does not," she said. "And it does not matter to me at all. But I suppose you might have considered this before coming here."

"I should have, yes, or I should have more carefully," he said. "But perhaps it was the brandy doing the considering. I am sorry."

"Your coat is on the chair," Lucy said, matter-of-factly. "I'll take the glass, thank you." She then saw him to the door and shut it behind him.

"Oh, you gallant cavalier," she said, her voice dripping with contempt. **"Ready one moment to take advantage of a poor girl like me, and then overcome with scruples."**

"Jezebel!" he cried. "Do you think I would betray my suffering wife for a mess of pottage?"

"You have betrayed her already!" she said, with her eyes blazing.

With her right hand she reached for the dagger in his belt, removed it, and plunged it into his heart. "I may hang, but you will betray no more women!"

Lucy was reading the final lines as Cora entered the room. She thought the scene quite satisfactory.

"They're sending a carriage in ten minutes," Cora said. "The bill is settled and they're sending a bellboy up. You look happy about something."

"I'll be happy when we're on the train," Lucy said. "Bring me one of the cherry lozenges, Cora."

To Frederick Douglass, with admiration and warmest regards. Here's to more cigars and brandy, Mark Twain. And then under it, *P.S.—You won the story contest.*

Frederick Douglass took a last look at the book, then packed it away carefully in his valise. It was morning, and he could hear Mrs. Tubman busying herself in the kitchen.

He had seen many a public meeting dissolve into shouts and fisticuffs. It was nothing new to him. Yet the previous night's events felt troubling in some new way, difficult to define. The fracas stemmed not from differences on policy, or even philosophy, but from something antagonistic to both, a vein of the irrational, something disintegrative.

The week-end was leaving him with an odd melancholy, as if

he had reached through a veil and just managed to put a finger on something important that floated away at the touch. A sense of connection that he had felt missing. Since his wife's death he had not known where to put himself. He maneuvered around a pit of loneliness and doubt, mainly by keeping busy. For all his traveling and lecturing, all the time away, all the gulf between their differing degrees of knowledge of the world, Anna had given him a center. All the energy that had gone into making Frederick Douglass . . . Yet when alone, who, indeed, was he? He thought of the lines he loved:

> Ye flowery banks o' bonie Doon,
> How can ye blume sae fair?
> How can ye chant, ye little birds,
> And I sae fu' o' care?

He rarely brought his violin when traveling, but he wished he had it now. At times of disturbance he would often concentrate on producing one lone, unwavering tone on the lowest string. The sound settled him, gathered the strands of his restless mind, pushed aside lists, correspondence, memories . . . as if here, in one place, all could be reconciled. . . .

A knock on the door of the bedroom; he answered, "Come in."

Mrs. Tubman opened the door. "You want something before you go? I've got porridge and coffee. When you're ready."

"Thank you, Harriet," Douglass said. "I'll be right there."

She nodded and closed the door.

Douglass bowed his head at the small writing desk there in the bedroom. He breathed deeply, tried to imagine that single tone. Time, he thought, to don the armor once again. . . . Then he rose and carried his bags out of the bedroom, placed them by the door, and sat down for breakfast.

Herman Melville had taken a seat by the window in the train's third coach and reflected back over the week-end with pleasure and satisfaction. In his valise were the first pages of the story of the handsome sailor. He had begun with an introduction, a poem he had written as a kind of overture, but which he was already thinking might be the coda to a story of inexplicable goodness encountering inexplicable malice, with the needs of the law and social continuity caught in the middle. The week-end had inspired him with its confrontations and juxtapositions.

Down the aisle he saw an old man carrying a bag, aided by a younger man, and as the pair drew closer he recognized Walt Whitman. At the same moment, Whitman recognized him, and asked if he might occupy the seat next to him.

"Of course," Melville said.

To the young man, Whitman said, "Thank you, Lemuel. Here; this is for you," and he handed something to him, which Melville assumed was money. Whitman cupped his two hands around Lemuel's hand and closed it around the gift, saying, "Thank you." The young man seemed to be struggling to say something, caught between gratitude, grief, uncertainty.

"Go now," Whitman said. "God bless you." Lemuel hesitated, then turned and walked toward the exit. He did not turn around.

Melville watched Whitman organize his belongings and settle himself, finally pulling a rumpled paper bag out of a satchel. "I hurt my hip last night. Here," he said, rummaging in the bag and pulling out a mandarin orange, which he handed to Melville. "These are delicious. I got them at the market yesterday." He pulled one out for himself as well.

And there it was again, Melville thought. The undeniable charm, the youthful disregard of formalities, the direct engagement . . .

what a unique man. "Thank you, Walter," he said. "Did you enjoy the week-end?"

"Oh yes," Whitman replied. A couple of drops of juice from the orange skidded down his beard and landed on his lapel. "Didn't you?"

"I did," Melville said. "Yesterday's program was quite revealing."

"I suppose," Whitman said. "People like to argue. Oh, look."

Down the aisle, passing their seat from behind, Forrest Taylor strode, carrying only a compact leather valise.

"I feel rather sorry for him," Whitman said. "His wife is ill."

Taylor continued into the next car, and as he crossed, he held the door open for a young-looking, red-haired woman who was entering. She noticed the two writers and immediately blushed, dropped her gaze to the floor, and sat in a seat near the door.

"Beautiful girl," Whitman said, reaching into his bag for another orange. "Would you like another?"

"No, thank you," Melville said. "It was delicious. I met her earlier, by the way."

"Whom did you meet?" Whitman said, peeling the rind.

"The young woman we just noticed."

"She's lovely."

"She's an aspiring poet," Melville said. "She approached me at the depot and gave me this." He held out a small, folded piece of paper, which Whitman took, after wiping his hands on his trousers.

Unfolding it, he read it silently for a moment, and then read it out loud.

> Each that we lose takes part of us;
> A crescent still abides,
> Which like the moon, some turbid night,
> Is summoned by the tides.

"It's beautiful," Whitman said. "May I copy it out?"

"Of course," Melville said. "I thought it was remarkable."

Whitman was extracting a notebook and pencil from inside his jacket.

"She asked if she might send me more of her work," Melville went on. "I felt badly to decline, but I am too old to be a mentor, I'm afraid."

Whitman did not respond; he copied out the words carefully into his notebook, making occasional low grunting sounds. Melville watched him with a mixture of affection and mild envy at a self-possession that he would never be able to claim.

"Thank you, Herman," Whitman said, replacing the notebook and pencil in his jacket and handing the paper back to Melville.

"Certainly," Melville said, replacing the folded leaf in his jacket pocket. He remembered walking into the auditorium for the afternoon panel the day before and seeing the others lined up on the stage, as if each were wearing a mask of himself, or herself. The public avowals would all be forgotten, and what would last? What they had made. Not what they argued for, but what they had proved. For all anyone knew, those four lines by that young woman, and any others she had in a notebook somewhere, might outlast all the debates, the angry broadsides and earnest proclamations made on behalf of this or that side of an issue . . . not the description, the advocacy, the case made, but the pure *thing*, brought into being. Or so he hoped for himself, at any rate.

"You know," Whitman said, breaking into Melville's thoughts, "I really did enjoy your *Typee*. I reviewed it for the Brooklyn paper, many years ago. I even remember the exact line I wrote—'As a book to hold in one's hand and pore dreamily over of a summer's day, it is unsurpassed.'" He paused for a moment, looking at Melville. "What is funny?"

"Nothing, truly," Melville said, wiping his eyes. "Forgive me, Walter."

"Forgive you for what? For laughing?" The train had just gotten under way. "I am so glad we met," Whitman said.

"And I, as well," Melville said.

It was entirely possible, Melville thought, that Whitman was the most guileless man he had ever met. One that might even stand on the gallows asking forgiveness for his persecutors.

And Whitman looked past Melville, out the window at the stores and houses of Auburn as they passed, and said, "What a delightful week-end this was."

—IV—

– 14 –

Delight is to him . . . who against the proud gods and commodores of this earth, ever stands forth his own, inexorable self. Delight is to him whose strong arms yet support him, when the ship of this base treacherous world has gone down beneath him.

IT WAS SATURDAY at the Auburn Boys' Reformatory, and I was delivering my weekly lecture.

Since my position at the Auburn Collegiate Institute was terminated I have managed to keep my lecturing skills in some kind of fighting trim here. It is, as always, difficult to keep my students' attention, and my current group is, if it were possible, even less engaged than my previous charges at the Institute. As far as they are concerned, Emerson, Whitman, and Twain might as well have written Greek, untranslated, and America might as well have been Australia. In any event it was the only teaching work I could secure without relocating completely, to God knows where, and the trustees of this institution seem to find some benefit in what they call "enrichment"—a somewhat grim terminological irony, as neither the students nor their instructor stand to gain any worldly riches from these lectures. And said trustees also pay me the dubious, but welcome, compliment of complete indifference regarding what I teach.

"What," I asked the class, "is Melville's Preacher saying, here? Who can tell me?"

They stared out the window, they drew anatomical pictures on their wooden desks, they passed notes back and forth. Occasionally there was a fistfight. Eventually, as always, it was time to wrap up, and I could barely get the words of dismissal out of my mouth before the students rushed the door.

That reporter, writing that I was "distraught." Who in my position would not have been "distraught?" That little item was an occasion for general mockery when it appeared. Let *them* try to organize that program. Then we would have seen who became distraught. . . . Apparently he moved to New York City to work for Pulitzer's scandal sheet. The perfect place for him . . .

Wickham Moreland, who had been nearly apoplectic in the aftermath of the disastrous final session, delegated Chairman Olander to terminate my relations with the Institute. This the chairman did with no excess of courtesy; the man who had been ready to kiss my hand for inviting Lucy Comstock had reverted to his accustomed posture vis–à–vis myself, and of that conversation I may at least say that it did not drag on too very long.

In any event, I have had ample time—too much time, perhaps—to revisit the conference in my mind. I take many long walks to fill the afternoons, longer and farther now than had been my wont in previous years. Once in a while, I see Mrs. Tubman in her barouche, on her way to sell pies, and she will nod in my direction. I can never quite tell if she recognizes me from that evening with Mark Twain and Frederick Douglass. It seems long ago. I am certain that I was the least memorable part of an otherwise memorable gathering.

What, finally, had it all meant? The conference had settled nothing. Was that what it revealed—a nothingness, which lived at the convergence of all these visions? Instead of answers, only more questions, and the barbarities remained, and the blindness, the forgetting, the greed. . . . What else remained? What were the lessons, after all? Did the nation's ideals amount to nothing more than shimmering rivers of words that vanished like mirages as soon as they ended? A nation that could conceive a Walt Whitman, a Mark Twain, a Frederick Douglass, surely promised more than that. The writers ignited a sense of possibility and self-creation. Was that, finally, their legacy? The promise that you could change, adapt, create something new and better, along with the nation as a whole?

And yet the same nation that conceived the breadth and scope of Whitman, the panorama of movement and personal reinvention in Twain, the moral reckoning in Douglass, the cautionary vision of madness in Melville, the supreme nobility of Lincoln—just as vigorously did it produce humbugs like P. T. Barnum, traitors like John Wilkes Booth, the greedy exploiters of every financial panic, and the vicious ringleaders of every lynching party . . . representative Americans all. After the discourse, the advocacy, the eloquence and rhetoric, the nation seemed destined to learn nothing and be doomed to repeat the same mistakes.

One day, rummaging through some clothes, I had found in a pocket an envelope with the word *Mockingbird* scrawled on the front; after a moment I remembered a distracted encounter with the red-haired woman who had given it to me as I tried to mount the stage for the final session. Inside it was a folded piece of paper with a poetic fragment, handwritten—

> Lad of Athens,
> Faithful be,
> To thyself, and mystery;
> All the rest is perjury.

Unsigned, and I was left to ponder the meaning. What was the perjury? Was it the dream of the perfectible society, the perfectible world? Was that perjury? And mystery . . . was America the mystery? Faith in the conundrum of the nation itself? Was America's emblem the grand polyphony, or the lone, burning voice? Many a night I lay awake, thinking about that woman. I wondered where she was, if I could find her. . . . I would have searched the Institute offices for a record of her registration, but I could not be sure that she had registered, and in any case I was not welcome even to set foot on the grounds of the Institute.

What had I expected of the writers? They came, collected their honoraria, moved on. What was left? The books. Why ask for more? Had they not contributed something indelible? The beauty residing in the quality of perception itself. Their eloquence hypnotized one into thinking they proffered answers, while they had only ever more fascinating ways of posing the question. And when they gathered all together at Midlake the room had unspooled, the mob overwhelmed it, as if the multiplicity of perspectives drove the audience mad. . . . Was it true of the nation as well? Was the madness the reality? Or was the noble ideal the reality? Or was it both? Somewhere, Douglass had called the Constitution a document "at war with itself," enshrining both the rationales for injustice and the means of dismantling the injustices it contained. Another answer to the question "What is an American?" Someone in an ongoing war with himself.

I walked, and I walked, and finally, at the end of the day, tired, I would return to my rooms, and by lamplight I would read Melville, or Twain, or Whitman. . . . I most often returned to the chapter titled "The Gilder," in *Moby-Dick*, those beautiful words about the seafarer:

Afloat all day upon smooth, slow heaving swells; seated in his boat, light as a birch canoe; and so sociably mixing with the soft waves themselves, that like hearth-stone cats they purr against the gunwale; these are the times of dreamy quietude, when beholding the tranquil beauty and brilliancy of the ocean's skin, one forgets the tiger heart that pants beneath it; and would not willingly remember, that this velvet paw but conceals a remorseless fang. . . .

And that same day, too, gazing far down from his boat's side into that same golden sea, Starbuck lowly murmured:

"Loveliness unfathomable, as ever lover saw in his young bride's eye!—Tell me not of thy teeth-tiered sharks, and thy kidnapping cannibal ways. Let faith oust fact; let fancy oust memory; I look deep down and do believe."

The belief *despite*—despite evidence, despite the certainty of disaster . . . the belief in possibility, even if one knew it to be impossibility . . . But there had to be possibility; wasn't the brilliant, beautiful surface just as real as the remorseless fang beneath? Surely there was a way forward. Whitman, Twain, Melville, Douglass, Stowe . . . I have their voices in my ear, and I cannot get rid of them. I still believe in America. God help me—I still believe in America.

— THANKS —

WITH GRATITUDE for friendship, encouragement, and aid along the way, to Zachary Lazar, Bill Driscoll, Noreen Tomassi, David Gates, Nina Girvetz, Roy Blount Jr., Lawrence Powell, Harry Shearer, Judith Owen, Jeff Rosen, Jonathan Santlofer, Sharon Guskin, Peter Alson, Steve Yarbrough, Collie Nelson, Steve Jungkeit, Sister Helen Prejean, Barry and Caroline Ancelet, John Howell, Stokes Howell, Deanne Stillman, and Julian Rubinstein. And to Elaina Richardson of Yaddo, and Sheila Gulley Pleasants of Virginia Center for the Creative Arts, for space and time.

A very special thank-you to Elvis Costello for believing in this book all along, and for his invaluable assist. And to Greil Marcus for pointing me in the right direction afterward.

Thanks to Jim McCoy and everyone at the University of Iowa Press for making a great home for *The Auburn Conference*.

No thanks will suffice for my agent, Henry Thayer, who has a heart of gold and nerves of steel. Thanks, as well, to everyone at Brandt & Hochman, especially Marianne Merola, Emily Forland, Lina Granada, and Gail Hochman.

To the memory of John Prine, who wanted to read this book. Land Ho, John.

To my mother, Lillian Piazza, who gave me my first copy of *Moby-Dick*, many years ago.

And, above all, to Mary Howell—for everything.